SOMEBODY TO LOVE

FAMILY MATCHMAKER
BOOK TWO

SUMMER COOPER

LOVY BOOKS

1

"What in the hell are we looking at?" Dana asked me. She was clearly bewildered by the billow of fog in front of us courtesy of the fog machines placed strategically around the small darkened theatre. And then there were the pyrotechnics that scared me every time a flame flared up a bit too close for my comfort. I kept patting my hair and sniffing the air, hoping a strand or two hadn't caught on fire. And, of course, there were the stage performers who went from sprouting poetry to doing back flips across the stage. Frankly, I didn't know what was going on.

"Clearly, it's art, Dana," I said, hiding a smile.

She frowned while her eyes stayed glued on a performer who was now stripping off his clothes in the middle of the stage while doing some sort of odd interpretative dance.

"Art? It looks like someone tried to recreate a Circque de Soleil performance but hired a bunch of high street artists."

That's exactly what it looked like as I watched one of the performers belly crawl his way across the stage. That performer was my boyfriend, Jerry. I had no idea why he was crawling across the stage, but I hoped it was part of the performance; otherwise, it would just be weird. Who was I kidding? ALL of this was weird.

"It's all very theatrical." I paused trying to come up with the right words. "It's supposed to be confusing… you know? Because it's so profound."

"It's not profound. It's dumb."

She was right. I smothered a giggle as I looked at Dana, my best friend since college. She was right; it was stupid, but I was trying to do my best to be supportive of Jerry.

He was an acrobat. A freelance acrobat he told me, and this was his first starring role in a theatre company which he co-owned with his best friend. I didn't know if acrobats had "roles" per se, but I knew this was really important to Jerry. And there was that little known fact that I had invested in his theatre company which was strangely doing really well. Before becoming a freelance acrobat, Jerry had been an accountant. I was pretty proud of him for pursuing his passion instead of doing the basic nine to five grind. I liked men who were different and as I watched Jerry, now wearing only his undies dancing across the stage like a Vegas stage girl, I couldn't have been prouder.

There must have been a look of pride on my face because I caught Dana staring at me with a look of bewilderment on hers.

"What?" I said, even though I knew where this conversation was headed.

"I just don't understand your taste in dudes, Piper." She shook her head and then gestured at Jerry who was now doing handstands, which wasn't very flattering given that all his goodies kind of fell down south in that position.

"Can't you just date an accountant or a school teacher?"

I made a face. "Jerry was an accountant. Operative word: *was*. He was bored to death. And a school teacher? Please."

I realized I shouldn't have been so dismissive in my reply once Dana shot me an annoyed look.

"Carter's a school teacher; well, at least he was. Remember? So you're saying your other best friend is boring?"

Carter was Dana's husband. The three of us had gone to college together and had been best friends all four years. Carter and Dana had always had a crush on each other, but they hadn't gotten together until years after college. And now they were happily married and had a total of three kids. One set of twins, who I think were toddlers or preschoolers now. I couldn't really tell—all kids looked alike to me. I could never tell one age from another. I frequently mistook six-year-olds for three-year-olds and vice versa.

And then there was my niece, Meredith, Dana's oldest daughter from her first marriage to my brother. Meredith was an absolute delight. I had loved that kid since I'd first laid eyes on her. They were just one big happy family: Dana, Carter, Meredith, and the twins. When I say that Dana and Carter were happy, I mean ecstatically happy. Dana was like a new person in comparison to who she'd been while married to my brother, Tom. The only good thing that had come from my best friend marrying my brother was my niece Meredith; otherwise, her marriage to Tom had been a waste of Dana's youth.

I felt that Dana had finally found herself, and I was so proud of her for following her heart instead of her head. I never followed my head when it came to romance, and I was fine. Just fine.

Finally, the lights came on and sporadic, hesitant applause sounded across the theatre as the audience exchanged confused looks. I owned one of those confused looks because I wasn't sure if the show was over or if this was some sort of intermission. They had an intermission earlier which had caught all of us by surprise because it included someone reciting poetry on stage which was part of, but not really part of the act. To be honest, it had just been weird. The show had only been interesting because we had no clue what was going to happen from one scene to the next.

Dana, upon noticing that the show was indeed done, stood up happily and made her way to the exit. I trailed behind her trying to keep up. A group near me murmured in excitement about how much energy and pizazz the show had. I figured they were art critics because, to be honest, the show kind of sucked to everyone but art critics.

When I caught up to Dana, she was shaking her head as if she couldn't believe what she had just seen. "Maybe I'm a cultureless soul, but give me Netflix over that any day."

"Dana, come on. You have to admit it was interesting." I had to defend my boyfriend, right? Even though it sucked?

"Interesting in the way that decaying vegetables are interesting. Like when you find a rogue, decaying vegetable in your refrigerator and you say to yourself, 'Is that a furry carrot or just a new form of mold?'"

"Are you comparing my boyfriend's show to mold?"

She thought about it and then said decisively, "Yep, I guess I am."

I reached out and tossed an arm around her shoulder. "That's why you're my best friend. I can always count on you to be painfully honest."

"I do my best."

"Don't I know it. Let's get a drink."

"We're not waiting for Jerry?" Dana asked as we headed for the exit.

I shook my head. "He said he needed to meet with the other investors—"

"Other investors?" She stopped and looked at me. "Piper, tell me you didn't."

I steadily kept walking, avoiding her eyes.

She raced to keep up with me, and it was only then that I realized I was practically running from the conversation I knew was inevitable.

"You invested in his company, didn't you?'

I shrugged. 'Maybe."

"Maybe. You can't sort-of-kind-of invest in something," She shook her head at me disapprovingly. "I wish you would have talked to me or Carter about this first."

"You guys would have just talked me out of it."

"Exactly."

Sighing, I opened the door to the bar a few doors down from the theatre. I was grateful for the crazy loud band playing up front. Now I could just have a drink in peace without worrying about a lecture.

As soon as we settled at the bar the band announced that they were taking a break and would be back soon.

Of course. I had the worst luck.

"So how much money did you give him, Piper?"

"Not much," I mumbled.

She gave me a skeptical glance. "Define 'not much'. Is that more than a hundred but less than a thousand?"

"Ummm…"

She shook her head in frustration. "Never mind. I don't want to know. "

For some reason, I felt terrible. I was an adult. I ran a successful translation company, and I had clients from three different continents. I could use my money any way I saw fit, but I felt guilty that I was funding yet another of my boyfriend's crazy plans.

I felt kind of like a pushover. Who was I kidding? I was a pushover. I was just too nice to say no to him. And he knew it. I guess deep down I felt taken advantage of, but I didn't think the person I loved would take advantage of me. At least, that was what I was convincing myself.

"It's fine. Really. I'm earning money from it already. So even though it probably wasn't my smartest move, at least it's not breaking me."

"That's not the point, and you know it."

"I invited you to have fun, not to be lectured about my life choices." I was angry now. And I rarely became angry, but I felt like the odd woman out. To be honest, Dana's life had been a mess before my brother divorced her. She had spent nearly a decade in a loveless marriage. And now she had the perfect family, the perfect husband, the perfect life.

And I suddenly felt like the odd man out. My two best friends had married each other, and now I was the sad friend who everyone felt sorry for. At least, that was what it felt like. I was "Poor Piper", who still couldn't get it together.

I guess Dana sensed my mood because she immediately became apologetic. "You're right, you're an adult. I'm sorry for trying to tell you what to do. You gave me plenty of great advice over the years that I never took, so I'm not sure why I would expect you to listen to me."

"Maybe because I'm not stubborn and determined to the point of misery. You know, the opposite of you."

"Yeah, that's probably it."

Our drinks appeared, and we both downed them. We started talking about nothing interesting when someone slid next to me.

The person touched me on the shoulder, and I turned around and found a young lady about eighteen sitting next to me. I was instantly confused. I didn't recognize her, and this bar wasn't for young adults really. At least, that was what I thought.

"Are you Piper?"

"Uh, hi, do I know you?" I turned completely to get a look at her.

She shook her head, and something about her eyes looked familiar. They were a strange light green with a hint of brown. Similar to Jerry's eyes.

"But that's your name? Piper, right? You're Piper? Jerry Lazarus' girlfriend?"

I instantly tensed. "Is Jerry okay? Did something happen?"

I started to stand up, when she abruptly caught me around my wrist, stopping any further movement.

I looked down at her hand and then back up at her. I didn't understand her expression. I didn't understand why she looked… furious.

"I'm Jessica," she said slowly, releasing my wrist. "You probably haven't heard of me, but I'm Jerry's daughter."

Jerry had a daughter? No. He had never mentioned a daughter. That couldn't be. This girl had to be wrong. This had to be some sort of ill-conceived prank. I frowned. "I don't understand… I—he—" I looked back at Dana who was staring between me and the girl, trying to figure out the next piece of the puzzle. Well, she wasn't going to find out from me, because I had no clue what was going on.

The girl nodded to herself as if my reaction finally confirmed what she already knew. Unfortunately, I was still very confused.

"I guess that means you've never heard of me. I figured that much." She slid from the stool but didn't immediately leave. She looked pensive as she grabbed her purse.

This clearly wasn't a prank. This lady was in pain emotionally. I could tell from her body language that she was doing all she could to not fall apart in front of us. Instinctively, I wanted to make it all better. "I'm sorry. I don't know why Jerry never mentioned you—"

"Maybe because he's still married to my mom," she said, looking up from her purse to deliver the verbal blow.

Stunned didn't began to explain how I felt. Dana didn't say a word, but she rested a hand against my arm. A silent sign of support.

"I'm sorry, I didn't know," was all I managed to get out.

The girl reached into her purse and took out a photo. She handed it to me and said, "That was taken last week at my high school graduation."

With shaky hands, I took the photo and confirmed it.

There was Jerry standing with a woman who was clearly the opposite of me in every way physically. She had red hair and was petite and curvy. They had their arms wrapped around each other and smiled toward the camera, while the young lady who stood before me now smiled widely in between them. Now I knew why her eyes looked so familiar. She had her dad's eyes.

"Which high school did you graduate from?" Dana asked. I wondered why she was making conversation while I was trying to process that I was an adulterer.

"Southlake Creek High," the girl said. "Why?"

"No reason."

"You think I'm lying or something?" Jessica shrieked. Her shoulders were tense and her breathing erratic. She was clearly getting more upset by the minute. I didn't blame her. If the roles were reversed, and I had been the one to find out that my dad was cheating on my mom, I would be unable to keep it together.

"Do you know where my dad is instead of being here with you?" She turned her now fiery gaze to me.

"He's meeting with some investors—"

"Investors?" She looked ready to cry. "He's such a liar. He's waiting with my mom for me to show up to dinner at a restaurant downtown."

I didn't know what to say. I was the other woman, and because of that I was causing this young lady so much pain. I felt terrible. I really did. It was a nightmare, and I desperately just wanted it to end.

"I believe you, and I'm sorry for all the pain I've caused you—"

She looked up at me as if she wanted to believe me, but just couldn't. Or rather she just wouldn't allow herself to believe that I wasn't some monster out to ruin the life she'd thought she had. We were both victims here. We had both been deceived and lied to. God, how I wished I had never laid eyes on Jerry Lazarus.

"I'm telling my mom tonight about you. She deserves better than my dad. I don't care if it ruins my family. But I just thought you should know that my father is a dirty liar who's screwing over the woman who stood by him when everyone including her own family said how much of a loser he was to quit his job. So, congrats," she said, giving me a wry smile as she tried to hold back tears. "I hope it was worth it."

I didn't know what to say as she marched away. I felt stunned, as if I had just been slapped. And then I felt Dana pulling at my hand.

"Let's get out of here."

In silence, I slid off the stool and made my way to the exit, trailing behind Dana, lost in thought. My stomach was topsy-turvy, and I knew at any moment that I would probably be sick. I told Dana to give me a second and made my way to the bathroom.

I went to the mirror and braced a hand on either side of the sink and told myself to just breathe. I wasn't a homewrecker. I did not date married men. I didn't. I wasn't that type of woman. Yet, suddenly I was. I believed the girl. What had her name been? Jessica? Yes, I could tell that it had hurt her to come here, to confront me. I readily believed everything she said. She had no reason to lie. And it wasn't her fault her dad was a no-good cheat. I felt dirty and cheap and a myriad of other unsavory feelings.

I forced myself not to cry, but I couldn't help the single tear that escaped. Frustrated, I swiped at it. I didn't deserve tears; I had been the other woman even if I hadn't known it. I had ruined a marriage, broken up a family. I was the worst of the worst. I cried, unable to hold back the tears. My parents' marriage had been crap, my brother was a serial cheater, and now I was an adulterer. It was like we as a family couldn't do anything right.

When I finally stopped crying, I washed my face and looked in the mirror at my bloodshot eyes. I wiped at them, but there was no use. Dana would know I had been in here crying. With a sigh, I made my way out of the bathroom. Dana was still waiting for me where I had left her in front of the other entrance door. When she spotted me, she rushed over and this time it was she who wrapped an arm around my shoulders.

"You okay?"

"No. I'm an adulteress."

She shot me a glance. "So you believe the girl?"

I nodded. "There's no reason for her to confront me and make up a lie unless she's some sort of crazy person."

"I checked Google. That high school did have a graduation last weekend, and Jessica Lazarus was one of the attendees. I even found a few of her social media pages —Instagram, Facebook, etc. And Jerry is in a lot of her pictures. In fact, he seems to be a very involved father."

I snorted. "Of course, he is. When he's not boinking some random woman who isn't his wife, he's daddy of the year."

"Well, I wouldn't go that far." Dana stopped me then, and it wasn't until that moment that I noticed we were standing in front of Dana's car.

We had ridden together to the show. She unlocked the door and I slid into the passenger seat, grateful for the reprieve.

I felt suddenly self-conscious. I didn't know why. No one else had overheard our conversation. But I felt as if the world had witnessed my shame.

"I had no clue he was married. I never suspected a thing. I feel so stupid. So, so stupid."

Dana sighed. "It's not your fault. Sometimes men are dicks. Just be glad you found out now and not seven years into your marriage."

I swallowed. Dana was talking about her previous marriage. I still felt guilty about Dana's marriage to my brother Tom. Tom had cheated on Dana while we had been in college, and I had never told Dana. At the time, I had thought that she wouldn't have believed me. When she found out years later that I had known about Tom's infidelities but hadn't told her, it had almost meant the end of our friendship.

I hadn't a clue if Tom had cheated on Dana while he was married to her, but it wouldn't surprise me if he had. He was my brother, but we had never seen eye to eye. He had always been an entitled jerk, playing with the emotions of others, so it hadn't come as a surprise to me when he ended up leaving Dana for a nineteen-year-old named Becca. Ironically, Becca had pulled a fast one on Tom and had left him not even a year into their marriage.

Tom hadn't remarried. He was living in Miami now working in real estate. Or maybe he was a producer? I couldn't keep up with his career changes or his questionable lifestyle decisions, not that I wanted to.

"Do you think his wife knew? Oh god, how do you think his daughter found out? Do you think she's been following him around the whole time?" I had so many unanswered questions circling my brain.

Dana shrugged. "Doesn't matter. And you'll probably never know. Tom never admitted to cheating on me while we were married, but you and I both know that he did. And often."

"I feel so stupid."

"Why?" Dana said, taking the nearest exit to my home. "You didn't know. So don't blame yourself." Dana paused and then said half to herself, "Unless you saw some warning signs and ignored them." She stopped at a light, turned a concerned gaze on me, and said, "Tell me you didn't. Tell me you didn't see signs and just ignore them."

I shook my head as I thought back to my relationship with Jerry. We had only been dating six months. And I hadn't noticed anything weird about him.

"I mean, he always came back to my place. I never once went to his. Is that a warning sign?"

"Umm… yeah. What was his excuse?"

It was my turn to shrug. "He said he was embarrassed of his apartment, that it was disgusting, and he didn't want me over there. He said his roommate was a slob."

"Well, your first error was dating someone in his thirties who still has a roommate, and your second error was not realizing that his secret roommate was really his wife and kid."

I winced. "What should I do? It's not like I can send her a card with an apology. And should I confront him?"

"I would love to throw something in his face or punch him in his nether region, but I'm sure that's assault. So maybe we shouldn't confront him."

"Not WE. Me."

"What? And miss out on all the action? No way. If

you're confronting Jerry, the no-talent cheater, then I'm going too."

I looked at Dana and knew she was serious. But I just couldn't bring myself to do it. I wasn't the confrontational type unless I was defending someone I loved. No. I would just move on. Forget about Jerry.

As if reading my mind, Dana said, "Actually, maybe confronting him is a bad idea. It seems like his daughter will probably handle that for you. And you don't want to be in the crosshairs if his wife shows up and sees you."

I nodded. "I need better taste in men."

"No kidding."

"Hey!"

Dana laughed as she pulled up in front of my house. It was a small, cute home in an up-and-coming neighborhood. I loved it. And I always felt proud when pulling up to it. It was my home, and I had done a lot of the remodeling on my own.

Dana parked the car and looked at me. "I'm sorry that this happened. For what it's worth, I know what that feels like and I'm really sorry that happened to you. Jerry's a dick. Also, you should probably get tested since maybe you weren't the only one he was playing hide the sausage with."

I winced, but I knew she was right. And there was one other thing. I had booked us a long weekend at a fancy hotel near a bunch of lakes since Jerry loved watersports. Now I had a super-luxe hotel room for a weekend and no one to take. And if I cancelled now, I wouldn't get any of my money back.

I mentioned it to Dana, figuring that she would jump at the chance to do something fun.

Dana frowned. "I would love to take it. I really would, but with Carter and the twins and Meredith—" She stopped suddenly and then said, "Take Meredith. She's been dying to get out of the house and do something fun, and she's on spring break next weekend."

"You think she wants to spend spring break with her crazy aunt?"

"Better than spending it with her boring parents and annoying siblings."

"She called you guys boring and the twins annoying?"

"Never out loud. But I have a sneaky feeling."

I laughed and shrugged. "That's totally understandable." I reached out and hugged Dana. She grunted and said, "That's a little too hard. I can barely breathe."

"I'm sorry. I just want you to know that I appreciate you. If it weren't for you being there in the bar, I probably would be a sobbing mess right now."

She pulled away and shrugged. "That's what friends are for."

At that moment I didn't feel like I even deserved a friend. I felt lower than low. I didn't tell Dana I was silently beating myself up. I felt ashamed, embarrassed, hurt. I just wanted to go into a dark closet and live there. How could I have missed all the signs? Or had I been deliberately obtuse and just ignored them all? Had I put my own search for happiness above what was right? I didn't want to think that I was THAT kind of person, but maybe I was. And now my selfishness had hurt someone. More than hurt someone—my selfishness had broken up a family. The thought made me feel sick.

I said goodnight and then slowly made my way to my front door. I opened the door, tossed my keys on the table in the entryway, slammed the door in frustration and then collapsed face first on my couch.

The tears didn't come immediately, but with my face in the pillows I finally let myself cry. I didn't like crying in front of anyone, even my best friend.

And when I was finally done crying I picked up my phone and noticed he had texted me. I felt too sorry for myself to be angry, so I read his text.

It simply said, "Hey, where you at?"

I knew the mature thing would be to just ignore him, but I was finally starting to feel something other than shock and shame. Finally, I was feeling anger.

"I'm home. How's the family?" I texted back.

A few minutes later my phone beeped and I looked at the text, "What are you talking about?"

"I met your daughter today. She looks just like you."

I sat on my couch, hoping he would deny it. I didn't doubt the young lady, but deep down I hoped it was all a misunderstanding. I didn't want to be the bad guy in this story. I didn't want to be the person Jessica Lazarus thought I was: a homewrecker, an adulterer, a liar. When my phone didn't buzz again, I knew everything I heard was true. Jerry was addicted to his phone. He'd seen my text. He didn't respond because there was nothing to say.

Feeling like a cheap castoff, I buried my head under a throw pillow, closed my eyes, and went to sleep.

2

"Auntie Piper, this is going to be the best vacation ever."

"Sure is," I said with false cheer. I was a loser. The biggest loser. I was going on vacation with my niece because the man I had trusted was a cheating asshole.

"Sorry about your boyfriend. Mom said he was a big loser."

Pretending it was no big deal, I just shrugged and kept my eyes on the road. "Yep. That's putting it lightly."

"Is it true he has another family?"

"Who told you that?" I narrowed my eyes at her. "Have you been eavesdropping on your mom's conversations again?"

"Maybe. Well, yes." She was honest to a fault. "I sort of overheard Mom telling Carter. So yeah."

I didn't bother to get angry. I wasn't really the angry

type. I was easy-going in nature, carefree even. Plus, it wasn't like Meredith planned to post my disgrace online somewhere. I was free to wallow in shame without the world knowing that I was a disaster at love.

"Thanks for coming with me, kid," I said, hoping to change the subject without any resistance from Meredith.

Gratefully, she obliged. "No problem. Plus, I really needed to get out of the house. The twins are driving me crazy. Who knew siblings would be so much work? I know babies don't come from storks, but if they did I would totally send the twins back with them."

I smothered a giggle. Meredith had always been a precocious little girl, and I thought it was hilarious how she talked about the twins as if they were her children instead of her siblings; as if she was the one responsible for feeding, clothing, and taking care of them. She sounded like a long-suffering single mom. I tried not to laugh.

"Being a big sister sounds tough." I figured why not play along.

She sighed deeply. "They keep me up twenty-four seven."

"Such a hard life for an older sibling."

"You have no idea."

I smothered another laugh, and then we were both

lost in thought. I didn't know what Meredith was thinking of, but the scenery grabbed my attention.

We were traveling through the mountains, but had descended into a valley area. Nothing but forest stretched out around us as far as the eye could see. It was a beautiful sight: radiant green that stretched on for miles. I had visited the rain forest in Brazil when I had lived abroad, and that was probably the only place on Earth that could possibly compare to the beauty that was around us now.

And just when I had thought the beauty around me was something I would never forget. The trees disappeared and a gigantic lake with the sun in the distant horizon greeted us.

"Wow," Meredith whispered. It was definitely a wow moment. "This place is beautiful. It's too bad your boyfriend sucked, because this place must be so romantic for couples. Maybe Mom and Carter can come here for their next anniversary."

As Meredith planned her mom and stepdad's next kid-free getaway, I tried not to get too depressed. Yeah, I hadn't had a functional relationship in a long time, but that didn't mean my romantic situation was hopeless, right?

Sometimes I felt my whole family was cursed to have bad relationship after bad relationship. My parents had been miserable in their marriage. My brother couldn't make a relationship work. And then there was me: hopeless at love.

I hadn't wanted that to be me. I wanted the whole fairy tale. I wanted the elusive happily-ever-after. And I was proud of myself for never settling, but I couldn't help but wonder why all my relationships failed. Was it me? Was it them? Was it both of us?

I thought about seeing a therapist, but I was way too cheap to pay someone to listen to my problems. I figured that's what Dana and Carter were for.

My thoughts shifted to the lake in front of us as the GPS navigated us to a large hotel right off the lake that had several other smaller hotels in its vicinity. It was like a little magical town hidden from the rest of the world. *Yeah*, I thought to myself, *this will be a great place to decompress.*

I pulled up to the large hotel, and Meredith and I piled out. There was a valet, and he quickly took my keys and had someone else grab our luggage. I smiled in gratitude. Once inside, Meredith and I exchanged impressed glances.

"This place is awesome."

I nodded and the receptionist gave us a broad smile. "I take it you haven't stayed here before?"

"Are we that obvious?

"Yes," he said, "but in a sweet way."

I gave him my information and he entered it into the system, searching for our names from the guest list.

Meredith began to twirl around in circles, trying to take everything in while saying "wow" over and over. The hotel reminded me of a log cabin, but obviously a fancier version. The entire hotel was an architectural wonder as far as I was concerned with all its fancy wooden surfaces and glass walls.

"Wow, indeed."

The host handed us our room keys and together, Meredith and I looked for our room.

"This is awesome," she kept saying over and over and once I found our room and opened the door. I thought so too. Suddenly, I didn't feel like such a loser. I felt kind of liberated.

"You're smiling," Meredith said in a sing-song voice.

I knew she was right, but I was feeling contrary.

"Yeah, I'm smiling… and what?"

"I thought you were going to be boring and down in the dumps all day."

"Well, fooled you. I'm fine. Perfectly fine."

"So what exactly happened with your boyfriend?" she asked, sitting down on the bed.

"Nothing that would interest you, just boring adult stuff," I said, checking out the kitchenette and bathroom. Everything was spotless and luxurious with a rustic feeling.

"Boring, huh? Really? You expect me to believe that?"

"Really."

"So why did you guys break up?"

"Because I didn't like him anymore."

"I don't believe you."

"Well, I don't know what to tell you, kid."

"Did he cheat on you?"

I didn't want to lie to her, but I also didn't know what to say.

So I said, "Let's talk about something else. Want to head to the lake or pool?"

She looked like she wanted to argue, but it was too late. I had already won. We had both seen the pool on the way in and even though the lake was beautiful, the indoor pool was tempting too.

We didn't even bother to unpack. We just tossed our bags on the beds, found our swimsuits, and then decided to head to the lake first.

According to what I'd read online, all the supplies were free to hotel guests. So when Meredith and I arrived at the lake, we had our pick of canoes, kayaks, jet skis and a host of other supplies needed for every water-sport I could imagine.

Of course, Meredith wanted to do the water skis. I promptly told her no.

"You should reconsider. It's a ton of fun," said a voice behind us.

I turned and looked behind me, and standing there was a man who looked like a minor Greek god.

"I'm Brock," he said, offering his hand as he smiled down at me.

I took his hand, looking up at him in unmasked adoration. He was at least six-four. His hair was sandy blond and his eyes very blue. At first glance, I would say he wasn't the kind of guy that I typically dated because he was just so darn beautiful. He was clean shaven and wearing nothing more than a pair of shorts that rode low on his hips. He looked like a surfer, like he belonged in Southern California. I wasn't sure if that was where surfers lived or not, but that sounded right.

But I didn't care where he was from. Yikes, he was hot. So hot that I wanted to cover Meredith's eyes.

"Are you a model or something?" she asked for the both of us.

Brock looked around and frowned. He seriously didn't know that she was talking to him. Wow, he was hot and not full of himself. I figured he must be taken or gay, or a combination of both.

"You do look like a model," I offered, finally finding my voice.

He looked embarrassed by my words, which I found so charming. And then that's when I noticed I was still holding on to his hand. *Oops*, I thought to myself, and promptly pulled my hand away.

Now that his hand was free, he rubbed his hand through his hair and said, "Not a model. Far from it. I'm a librarian."

Instantly, he piqued my interest with that mention alone. Wasn't I just saying to myself that I was done dealing with silly, flighty men? And look what had practically landed my lap: an Adonis with the world's most boring career.

I bet he wouldn't be caught dead running around a stage wearing only boxer shorts while doing weird interpretive dances. I bet he didn't breathe fire or know any magic tricks. In short, he was the opposite of every guy I'd dated or had wanted to date.

I felt it was a sign from the universe, so I quickly turned on the charm.

"So you're into watersports? What would you recommend for newbies?"

He pondered the question for a second and then turned that brilliant smile on me. "Kayaking is my favorite. I used to whitewater raft in college, though, so I'm partial to that too, but wouldn't recommend that to beginners."

"So you're into whitewater rafting? Did you go to school around here?"

"South Carolina."

"I could hear the tinge of a Southern accent."

"Really? I grew up in California."

"Ha ha," Meredith said dryly, clearly enjoying my failure at flirting.

I shot her a look and said, "Well, see you around. I think we'll try canoeing," as I pulled my niece away.

"Oh man, I wanted to go water skiing."

"Can you even ski?" I said, turning away from Brock.

She ignored my question and shot me a look of pity. "You didn't even tell him your name," Meredith whispered loudly. "How are you going to get him to date you if he doesn't even know your name?"

The last sentence was said in a rather loud whisper, and I just wanted to disappear. Maybe bringing Meredith wasn't the best idea.

"Meredith, shhhh—"

Meredith rolled her eyes and turned back to where Brock was standing, untying one of the docked boats. "She's Piper, by the way. That's her name. Piper. I think it's a pretty cool name," Meredith said to Brock, who just looked at her and then me in confusion. "And she's not my mom. She's my aunt. And she's single. Just in case you were wondering. Like she doesn't have a boyfriend at all. She's super single."

For the second time in two minutes, I just wanted to disappear.

And as if the embarrassment wasn't enough, Meredith continued, "Why don't you come with us,

Brock? You can show us how to do this canoeing thing. I'm Meredith, by the way."

Brock looked taken aback. I guess a child's forwardness wasn't something he had experienced before.

I immediately shot Meredith a look. "What?" she said, pretending to be innocent. "Don't you think he's cute?" she said in a stage whisper.

I hooked an arm around her shoulders and told Brock we would see him around.

"You're infuriating," I said with a laugh when we far enough away so that he couldn't hear us.

"If by infuriating, you mean super useful, then yep." She looked over her shoulder, peered at him, and said, "So do you think he's married?"

I knew there was no way that Dana would have discussed my love life, or lack thereof, with Meredith, but there was always a chance she might have overheard something about Jerry being married. After all, I had called Dana and Carter to complain about how much of a loser I was. Maybe Meredith had heard a little bit of my plight. I wasn't sure how much more embarrassing life could get.

I sighed and replied, "I don't know."

"I didn't see a ring."

"True. Thanks for checking."

"No problem."

We spent the rest of the afternoon hanging out. We

kayaked. We canoed. We even rented pedal boats and had a great time going around in circles, neither one of us were very effective leaders, apparently. I didn't know I could feel so depleted by being out in the sun. Around the time the sun was setting, we were both exhausted having spent the whole day on the water.

Meredith promptly fell asleep once we got back to our room. I tried to take a nap too, but I was a terrible napper. Bored, I decided to pick up a sandwich from the deli I had noticed near the front desk. I took a look at Meredith. She was fast asleep. I assumed I would only be gone for a few minutes. I locked the door and made my way to the deli.

I was bending down staring at the different sandwiches available. They all looked good, or maybe I was just hungry. After all, Meredith and I had skipped breakfast and forgotten about lunch because we had both been having too much fun to think about food.

"Hmmm, avocado sounds delicious…. or do I want turkey?"

"I'm partial to the avocado, actually," said a voice behind me.

I turned around partially and smiled. Immediately, I straightened up. It was Brock. He smiled back at me.

"Or you could try to mix it up, maybe have a little turkey with avocado on the side."

"That sounds good," I said, smiling at him. He really

was a beautiful man. This time he had on a shirt, and I felt a little disappointed.

To my surprise, he caught me checking him out and immediately called me out on it. "I decided to join civilization and put on clothes."

"I got to admit, I prefer you uncivilized."

He grinned. "That could be arranged."

"A flirtatious librarian… and people say librarians are boring."

"Trust me. I'm definitely not boring." He leaned on the counter and said, "So where's your precocious niece?"

"Sleeping."

"There's a kids' club here at the hotel, you know. Maybe you can let her enjoy herself there and we could get a drink later on tonight?"

"I think she would approve of that…"

"I would think so too, since she seems to be concerned about you being super single."

We both laughed, and I reached for my sandwich. "Put it on my tab, Sinclair," he said to the cashier who nodded. He was on a first name basis with the cashier? I guess Brock was a very friendly person or he visited often.

"Thanks for the sandwich, and I guess I'll see you tonight."

"How's eight?"

"Works for me."

"Eight it is," he said, turning away from me.

I walked away with pep in my step. I was doing great. I was asked out by probably the hottest man on Earth. Things were certainly looking up.

I made my way back to my room where I found Meredith watching TV.

"A sandwich? Great. I'm hungry."

I handed it over and ignored the growling of my stomach. Meredith quickly began to devour it.

"So why do you look so happy suddenly?"

I threw myself back on the bed. "I have a date."

She gave a squeal and tossed her sandwich on the bed and began jumping up and down. "Yes. Yes. Yes. Was it the guy with no shirt on? He liked you. I knew it."

"His name is Brock, and I think he likes me too."

"Of course he does." She then bit her lip. "But if you're going on a date, what am I supposed to do?"

"There's a kids' club."

"Tell me more."

I laughed and said, "I know nothing about it."

She flopped down on the bed and reached for the pamphlets they had given us.

"Well, there's nothing about it here. Or here. Or—ha. Found it."

She began to read it out loud, "There's a climbing

wall, a mini-golf area, laser tag, free pizza—oh my gosh, FREE pizza. I'm definitely going."

I laughed. "You sure?"

"Yes," she said excitedly, "I'll have pizza and you'll have boring adult food, like salmon." She made a face, and I couldn't help but giggle. "Okay, so let's get you dressed. You have to wear something sexy."

A few hours later, I was dressed in a Meredith-approved outfit. I had on a mini-skirt and a flowery crop-top. Meredith had great taste. I had dropped her off at the kids' club, and she had quickly waved goodbye to me to go greet a group of pre-teens waiting to climb the rock wall.

I then made my way to the little restaurant where Brock wanted to meet me.

He was already there when I arrived and like a gentleman, he stood up as I approached. He had changed his clothes and now wore lose-fitting khakis and slim-fitting white shirt. He looked like temptation on two legs.

"You look so cute," he said to me as he pulled out a stool at the bar. I smiled up at him and slid onto it.

"Did you order a drink without me?" I asked, gesturing to the drink in front of him.

"I was a little nervous, so I needed some liquid courage."

"I make you nervous?"

"You're beautiful, funny… so therefore intimidating."

"You must not get out much."

"I'm a librarian," he joked. "I keep my nose stuck in a book."

I appraised him quickly, taking note of his large biceps and expansive chest. "There's no way you got that body by reading books all the time."

"I read really heavy books."

I couldn't help but laugh.

The bartender came by and asked me for my order. I ordered a beer, and Brock shot me a look of approval.

"So what are you doing here all alone, Piper? By the way, I love your name. It's so different. You have no idea how many Jessicas I've dated."

God, of all names, did he have to use the name of Jerry's daughter. I pushed that thought away and smiled at Brock. "I hated my name growing up for that very same reason, but then I got older and embraced being different."

"Being different is definitely not a bad thing."

"I'm older and wiser."

"Cheers to being old and not as stupid as in our youth."

Brock was funny. We touched our glasses together and settled into what I considered first date chit-chat. He told me about where he was from, and I shared a few important details about my life.

Brock was interesting, clearly well-read. And it seemed everyone was fond of him. A few of the employees stopped by just to say hi as we talked. He introduced me to a few of them.

I felt like I was finally making a connection.

"So what are you doing here alone?"

"I originally booked this place for me and my boyfriend—"

"Oh, so you're attached," he said with disappointment written on his face.

"Ex-boyfriend," I corrected. "At least now he's my ex. When I booked this place, we were together and then I found out he had a wife and a kid."

"What? Like an ex-wife?"

"No, like a current wife. I was confronted with the truth after one of his performances."

"His show? What was he an actor or something?"

"Or something. I'm not sure if what he was doing could be called acting."

Brock frowned. "He wasn't like a stripper or porn star or something, was he?"

"What? No," I giggled. "What made you say that?"

"I don't know. My mind's in the gutter."

"I didn't think librarians talked about porn."

"Are you kidding me? Most of my job is spent telling people to stop watching porn on the public computers in the library."

"You're kidding me? Young people are that bold nowadays?"

"Young people? Oh, the porn viewers aren't teenagers usually. These are mostly men and women in their forties."

"Yikes. Women too?"

"Equal opportunity porn."

I laughed hard, and he joined me.

He looked at his watch and said, "Listen, I know you can't be away from your niece long, so why don't we just exchange numbers now and catch up later on this week?"

"That sounds good," I said.

He handed me his phone, and I programmed my number in. As I handed his phone back to him, I caught him looking at my legs.

He gave me a boyish grin. "I was trying to be a gentleman, but those legs of yours are making it crazy difficult."

His thigh was pressed against mine, and I could feel the heat of his body. If Meredith wasn't my roommate, I was sure my night with Brock wouldn't be coming to an end.

"I guess I'll see you later," I said, sliding reluctantly off the stool.

He caught my hand and said, "If I had it my way, this isn't how this evening would end."

My pulse quickened as he leaned toward me and kissed me. It was unexpected, but didn't matter. I responded instantly by wrapping my arms around his neck, bringing him in closer until my breasts were pressed against his chest. And then, just like that, he abruptly pulled away.

"We're definitely going to have to do that again. Call me."

And with that, he walked away and I stared after him. The bar was still empty, but I felt super self-conscious suddenly. I had just made out with a stranger and maybe years ago, I wouldn't have cared, but as an adult I was slightly embarrassed.

In that moment, I couldn't tell which emotion felt stronger, my embarrassment or my lust. It didn't matter, because at least I was officially over Jerry. I laughed to myself, that had only taken about a week.

"You seem happy," were Meredith's first words to me when I went to pick her up from the kids' club.

"So do you," I said to her and it was true. She looked exhilarated when I found her climbing down the rock wall.

"The rock wall was awesome," she admitted. "I can't wait to do it again. Can I go to kids' club tomorrow? Pleaseeeeeee… and you can go out on a date with Brock again." She twisted from side to side, barely able to contain herself.

"Fine," I said with a long-suffering sigh, as if it was such a big sacrifice to agree to go out with the world's hottest man again. "Since you're twisting my arm, fine."

We picked up dinner and headed back to our room. When Meredith was finally asleep on the sofa bed, I couldn't help but wonder to myself if I was making yet the same mistake again. How well did I know Brock? But then I told myself that I was being silly. Not every guy was a douchebag. Right? Just all the guys I liked. With that in mind, I fell into a restless sleep.

BROCK SAT across from me in the large dining room, handsome in a blue button-down shirt. His hair was slicked back, and he had let a little bit of his beard grow in. It was our third and final day at the resort, and I wondered what would happen after I left.

Would he keep in touch? Would we both just go our separate ways?

I didn't want to be presumptuous. What if he wasn't interested in anything more than a fling? Not that we had had a fling. Besides a few heated kisses, nothing had really happened between us. *Maybe that would change tonight,* I thought to myself, eyeing him from underneath my eyelashes.

Feeling naughty, I wiggled my foot out of one shoe and traced my foot up his leg.

He jumped, startled, and I let out a bark of laughter. "You okay over there?"

"You know what you did."

I smiled innocently. Feeling bold, I said, "Why don't we go back to your room? My niece will be at the kids' club for another hour."

"I've been dying to hear those words." He stood up and offered his hand to me. I took it, and he tossed a few twenties out of his wallet onto the table.

He held my hand as he escorted me to the elevator. As soon as the doors closed, he backed me against the wall of the elevator door, and I let his hands go up my skirt. He didn't waste any time as his hands slid under my panties and grabbed my behind. He squeezed my ass and then brought his mouth down on mine, kissing me hard as he picked me up and wrapped my legs around his waist.

He pressed his sex against the heat between my legs and I rotated my hips, rubbing against it, wanting to feel him pressed against me. I felt like every encounter we had up until this moment had been foreplay. I was done with foreplay. I wanted the real thing.

The elevator began to slow, marking our impending arrival, and he groaned in disappointment. He quickly let me go, and we sprung apart at the last minute as a passenger climbed on.

"Good evening," the older woman said as she

entered. She stood in front of us facing the elevator door.

I grunted a hello and tried not to gasp when I felt Brock's hand making its way back up my skirt. I hit at his hand and admonished him in a whisper.

He gave me a boyish grin and pinched my ass. I tried to swallow my squeal, but apparently the other passenger heard me and turned quickly in our direction. I tried to look innocent, while Brock said, "Must have been the elevator. It's old, you know. It squeaks sometimes."

"Hmmm," was all the older woman said as she turned away from us, expressionless. I shot Brock a glare and he leaned down and kissed me softly on the lips. That served to shut me up immediately.

Finally, the elevator stopped again and the woman got off and surprised me as she turned around and said, "Have fun, you two."

I blushed, and Brock chuckled. As the elevator doors closed, he wrapped his arms around my waist and pulled me toward him. "Now, where were we—?" he said as he began kissing my collarbone, as his hand found its way to one of my breasts.

Gasping, I slapped at his hand and hissed, "Not in the elevator. There are cameras. Behave yourself."

"You didn't ask me to behave myself earlier," he said as he kissed my ear, and I shuddered. This time when the elevator doors opened, I was in too much of a sexual daze to notice. It wasn't until Brock was pulling at my hand and leading me out that I even realized we were out of the elevator.

He led me to his room, opened the door quickly, and didn't bother to turn the lights on as we tore at each other's clothes.

His kissed my nipples without removing my dress, making me moan as his warm mouth moved over the material. I could only imagine how his lips would feel on my nipples without my clothing. I pulled at his pants, trying to undo his zipper, while he tried to unzip my dress.

And just like that we lost our balance and tumbled onto his bed. I landed on top of him and became the aggressor, kissing him, while trying to tug his pants down, and that's when my phone rang.

I stopped immediately to answer it. Who would be calling me at this time of night?

"Don't answer it," Brock said. I couldn't see his face in the dark, but his voice was thick with desire. I shimmied off him trying not to notice how hard he was as I slid my body off his.

"I have to answer it," I said, still breathless. "It could be Meredith."

Quickly, I reached for my purse, answered the

number which I didn't recognize and said, "Hi, this is Piper."

"Hi, umm, Ms. Piper, we have your niece here, Meredith—"

"Oh my god, is she okay? I'll be right there—"

"She's okay. We think she might have hurt her ankle though. Can you come get her? We're in—"

"I'll be right there," I said, reaching for my purse and forgetting completely about Brock.

"Wait, where are you going?" he asked, climbing off the bed as I opened his hotel room door.

"Meredith hurt herself, I have to go. I'll call you—" And with that, I sprinted down the hall and didn't even bother to wait for the elevator. I found an exit sign and sprinted down the stairs as fast as I could go.

In a matter of minutes, I was on the same floor as the kids' club. I found Meredith at the entrance looking bummed.

I instantly kneeled in front of her. "Honey, are you okay?"

She nodded. "I told them not to call you. It's just a little sprain. Look I can walk fine."

She stood up, took two wobbly steps, and then almost collapsed. I caught her and steadied her weight against me.

"Hold on to me. We're going home. Well, first, we're going to a hospital and then we're going home."

"A hospital? It's not that serious."

"You can barely walk."

"I'm fine. I think I just twisted something."

The employee who managed the area piped up, "There's an urgent care about ten minutes from here. You guys could go there."

Grateful, I said as much and then helped Meredith hobble to the elevator. "How in the world did this happen?"

"One of the bigger kids ran into me. Practically ran me over."

"Did he apologize at least?"

"No," she said, and I could tell she was trying not to tear up. I knew the other kid didn't do it on purpose, but I still was too angry to speak.

"You're going to be fine." I brought her close to me and kissed her forehead. "I'm going to take care of you. You're going to be fine."

An hour later, we were out of the urgent care facility and making our way back to our hotel.

"See, I told you there was nothing to worry about," Meredith said for like the hundredth time. She had been right, although deep down I knew she had been worried too. She was fine. Her foot wasn't even sprained. But it was a little sore still from where the kid had connected with her.

"You should just call Brock and continue with your date. I can watch Netflix or YouTube in our hotel room."

"Nope. I'm not leaving you alone ever again."

"Oh, come on."

"Nope. Never. End of story."

"Fine."

She folded her arms and I felt a little bad that she was angry with me, but then I remembered that she wasn't my peer, she was my niece. It was my job to keep her safe and all that mattered was that she was safe. Even if she were mad at me.

I hated when she was mad at me though. "Hey, listen, I'll buy you a whole pack of Snickers if you stop being mad at me, deal?" I was such a pushover.

Meredith loved Snickers. "Deal," she said happily.

"I can't believe I'm bribing you with Snickers."

"Me neither. This is great."

Sighing to myself in resignation, I pulled up to the nearest gas station and was about to get out when Meredith grabbed my arm.

"Isn't that Brock?" she asked, pointing in the direction of the gas station's lobby which was clearly displayed courtesy of the windows that lined the building. It was definitely Brock. He was in the gas station buying a case of beer.

"Yeah, that is Brock—what does he need with a whole case of—"

I abruptly stopped as a woman appeared by his side. She leaned her chest against his arm and then stood on her tiptoes and whispered something in Brock's ear. He smiled down at her, and she smiled back. Clearly, she had whispered something naughty. She kissed him then, and I recognized her as one of the other hotel guests.

I was done. I'd seen enough. Feeling numb, I pulled out of the gas station. I could feel Meredith's eyes on me, but I didn't say a word. What could I say? I was an imbecile.

I was stupid. So stupid. Brock had been playing me the whole time. I bet his game was sleeping with women who came alone to the resort. A librarian. Ha. What a liar. What a dirty, dirty liar.

"Umm, Auntie, you're speeding."

Immediately, I slowed down and said softly, "Thank you."

She looked at me from the corner of her eyes and I sighed, "I guess I'll get you those candy bars tomorrow."

"It's cool," she said, looking again at me with concern. "Do you think that girl was his girlfriend?"

I didn't bother beating around the bush. "I've seen her around the hotel. I think that's his game. He dates all the single women who come here, sad and lonely. Gosh, I sure know how to pick them."

"It's not your fault," Meredith said. "Sometimes guys do stupid things."

"Yeah," I said softly. But I blamed myself. I had picked wrong, again. I held back tears. I didn't want Meredith to see me cry. Clearing my throat, I said, "Mind if we head back home tonight?"

"No. I kind of think we should."

"You sure you won't be upset?"

She shook her head. "I think we should just probably leave."

I didn't need any more convincing as I headed to the hotel, all the while trying not to get upset. First Jerry, now Brock. Why did I keep picking the wrong guy? Or better yet, why did the wrong guy always pick me?

3

"Thanks for taking Meredith with you. She had a great time," Dana said again for the billionth time. She had been thanking me for at least a week already.

"It's no problem. We had fun."

She side-eyed me and I knew she wanted to talk about what happened, but I was too embarrassed. I was sure Meredith had filled her in.

"Do you want to talk about it?"

"Nope. There's nothing to talk about."

"Well—"

"I have terrible taste in men. The end."

"It's not your fault."

"Yeah, it is. I keep picking them so the common denominator is me. I've accepted that."

"You're being too hard on yourself."

"Gosh," I said, throwing myself on her couch, "How many other married or taken men do you think I've dated? So far, Brock and Jerry? Maybe I'm a professional 'other woman' and just never knew it. Maybe my name and phone number are written on a bathroom stall somewhere: *For a good time, call Piper. She's too dumb to figure out if you're married or not.*"

"Stop it."

"It's the truth."

"Everyone makes mistakes like that, Piper."

"Oh really?" I said, shooting Dana a skeptical look. "So tell me, Dana, when's the last time you slept with a married man?"

"What, I would never do that!" she said quickly.

"Exactly."

"Piper, you know what I meant."

"I'm a loser. I should just give up on romance. From now on, it's just going to be me and my cat."

"You don't have a cat." She frowned. "You don't have a cat, right?"

"Doesn't matter. I'm bound to get multiple cats. That's my destiny. That's what spinsters do."

"You're not a spinster. You're too young to be a spinster."

I ignored her. "How many cats do you think are too many? Seven? Nine?"

"One. One is too many."

I gave her a fake frown. "You're cruel."

She settled down next to me. "Listen, I know you're upset and you have every right to be, but maybe you just need a little help with this whole dating thing."

"A little help? I need a ton of help. I don't know what I'm doing or, better yet, I don't know WHO I'm dating."

Dana hesitated and then handed me a little envelope. "Meredith wanted me to give you this for your birthday."

I looked at the envelope and frowned. "Why didn't she just give it to me?"

"Well, she didn't think you would be all that receptive to it, sooooo…" Her voice trailed off, and I frowned. Why would Meredith think that?

I opened the card and looked inside. *You can do it, Auntie. I believe in you.*

"I'm glad she believes in me, but what is she talking about? What can I do?"

And that's when I saw it. It was a username and password.

"What's this for?" I asked Dana, pointing to it.

"It's your birthday gift," Dana said, looking guilty.

Uh oh. "What kind of birthday gift?"

Dana began to look even guiltier. "Well, you see. Since you've had some trouble finding someone, Meredith decided that she wanted to help."

"Ummm okay…" I said, still not getting it.

"Meredith has this friend or enemy at school, depends on what day it is… anyway, Danny Schultz," Dana paused. "You remember Danny, right?"

"Kind of. The one with the wacky mom?"

"Yeah, well it turns out that she's no longer wacky. She met someone and is now kind of back to normal."

"And that has to do with me how?"

"Well since it worked for Danny's mom, Meredith thought it might work for you."

"What might work?" I still wasn't following.

"A dating service."

"A dating service? Hold on, are you saying my niece got me a dating service for my birthday?" I groaned and put my head in my hands. "Oh God, I'm pitiful. Did she save up all her allowance and buy me an eHarmony account?"

Dana laughed. "She wasn't trusting anything besides the service Danny's mom used. So she convinced me and Carter to help her pay for it. It was crazy expensive. Whoever owns it must be rich. Anyway, happy birthday. Go find a date."

She shoved a pamphlet in my hand and said something about going to check on the twins, and then she was gone.

I didn't know whether to laugh or cry. My niece cared so much about my love life she'd asked her parents to buy me a crazy extravagant gift. I couldn't accept this.

I stood up and looked for Dana. I found her with Carter.

"Nope," he said before I could say anything else. "She wanted you to have it. So you have to keep it."

"Come on, you guys; this is too much."

"Just keep it. Go out on a few dates. It will mean the world to Meredith. She just wants you to be happy."

"I am happy."

"Piper, you've been wearing that same pair of pants all week."

"Wearing the same clothes repeatedly is eco-friendly. I'm trying to conserve water on this planet."

"Lies. Try again."

"Come on, you guys. I don't want to go to a dating service. That makes me sound desperate."

"You should be desperate," Dana mumbled.

"Thanks for the vote of confidence."

Carter came over and sat down between us. "Look, Piper, just check out the website and see what the company has to offer. We have nothing to lose. It's a money back guarantee. And the dating service is reputable. Go meet with a dating specialist."

"A dating specialist? You have got to be kidding me?"

"Stop being such a Debbie-downer; that's my role in this friendship. You're supposed to be the risk taker. The fun one." Dana nudged me and gave me a teasing smile.

"I'm not having fun anymore, and I'm done taking risks with love," I said softly, and Dana's smile fell.

She reached out and squeezed my hand. "Love is a risk, hon. Don't give up on it just because you met some jerks. Imagine what my life would have been like if I had given up on love after being married to Tom. I wouldn't have three wonderful kids or my happily ever after with Carter," she said, gesturing to a family photo of all of them together.

I knew she was right. I just didn't believe in online dating or dating apps. Or mixing dating and technology. Despite being a millennial, I was old-fashioned. The thought of needing someone else's help to secure a relationship made me feel like the world's biggest loser.

"Is this some weird app that I have to download? You know the type where I have to scroll through millions of Photoshopped faces?"

"Nope. Not at all. It's all in person. They have an office downtown. I'll email you the info because we already went ahead and scheduled you an appointment."

"What?"

"You don't have to thank us," Dana said.

"What? I'm not." Thank them? I wanted to shake them, but that wouldn't be the nicest thing to do to people you've been best friends with for over a decade.

"It's tomorrow at eight am," Carter added.

"What?"

"One day you'll thank us."

I shook my head, but surprisingly, I felt gratitude that Dana, Meredith, and Carter had gone out of their way to help me find my happily ever after. I couldn't ask for better friends. No, they were more than friends. They were family.

"Okay, I'm in. Send me the info. But if I end up dating a crazy person, I'm blaming all of you."

Dana scoffed. "Are you kidding me? I saw Jerry's act. You couldn't date anyone crazier than him if you tried."

Knowing she was right, but not wanting to admit it, I said my goodbyes, thanked them for their generosity, and mentally prepared myself for asking a stranger for help with my love life.

4

───────

The next morning, I exited the swanky building where the dating service was located. It was called Infinity Connections. I thought the name was cheesy, but the service had been impeccable. The consultant who I met with, Sylvia, really knew her stuff. She had been easy to talk to and knowledgeable. After an evaluation that felt sort of like a psych test and a series of questions about me and my preferences, I started to feel as if she were a best friend or trusted counselor who I told my woes to instead of an employee of a dating company.

All in all, it wasn't as bad as I thought it was going to be. Yes, it had been embarrassing, but that was all my fault. I had made it clear that I didn't want to be there and had even said I didn't need the service. But then we started talking about my most recent relationships and since both ended with me probably being the other woman, it became clear to me and the dating specialist that I was deluding myself.

I figured that I would get myself a latte and then head back home to get back to work when my phone rang. I didn't recognize the number and started to just ignore it, when I remembered that the dating agency planned to call me regarding my first meetup with a potential match.

"Hi, this is Piper."

"Piper, thanks for picking up," Carter said, sounding frantic. Carter never panicked, so I knew immediately something was wrong.

"Carter?" I looked at my phone again to confirm that he wasn't calling me from his cell phone, "What number are you calling me from?"

"Work," he said shortly. He was the principal at a local private school in the area. "Meredith is participating in an event today, and there's supposed to be a party afterward."

"Okay." I was clueless why he was telling me this.

"Dana was supposed to chaperone the party, provide snacks; you know, the usual. But the twins are sick. Seems like the stomach flu is making its rounds."

"Ewww…"

"You have no idea. Anyway, so can you—"

"You don't have to ask. What time I should be there?"

"How about twelve?"

I looked at my phone and then confirmed mentally that I would have time to make myself look school presentable. "Sounds good, I'll be there early."

"Thanks, and don't forget. No nuts. No dairy. Preferably no gluten."

"Ummm… so that leaves me with what exactly? Air or fruit?"

"You're creative. I'm sure you'll think of something. Thanks again," he said, hanging up.

I stared at the phone wondering what in the world I was supposed to prepare in a matter of hours that wouldn't include nuts, dairy, or gluten.

I changed clothes, headed to the grocery store and wandered the aisles looking for something, anything. I wasn't coming up with any ideas, but the clock was ticking. I briefly wondered if I could just buy the kids a bunch of chicken nuggets from a fast food restaurant, but figured greasy little children wouldn't sit too well with their parents.

With a sigh, I grabbed a cooler, a bag of ice and all the fruit popsicles I could find. Unconventional, yes. But hey, the kids would love it.

"Having a party?" the checkout lady asked.

"Yep."

"An ice cream party?"

"Uhhh… yeah…" I frowned, wondering if I was

making the right decision. *It was too late now,* I said to myself as I paid the cashier and wished her a hearty goodbye.

I placed everything in my car and arrived thirty minutes early to Meredith's school. I was feeling pretty proud of myself until I remembered that the popsicles could easily melt. I needed to find a fridge and fast.

I grabbed the cooler, filled it with ice, placed the popsicles on top and wobbled unsteadily in my heels toward the entrance of the school. I felt moisture pooling on one side of the cooler and realized that there was a hole in it. Great. Just great.

I approached the school doors with a scowl on my face. I had the worst luck. A guard saw me coming and stopped me.

"Can I help you?" he asked.

"I'm here for the recital after party," I said, forgetting the real name of the event. I wasn't sure Carter had described it as an after party.

The guard held back a laugh, but couldn't conceal his grin. "After party? I didn't know we were running a club."

I laughed. "I'm old. Cut me some slack."

He smiled back. "I get it. I feel the same way. The party's in Great Room B. Go straight down the hall and then to your left. You can't miss it."

"Straight down the hall and then to the left. Got it."

I walked down the hall mindful of the trail of water I was probably leaving behind. I reached into my purse and tried to find some napkins. Of course, I didn't find anything. I started muttering to myself.

"This sucks so much. So, so much," I said, digging deeper and getting frustrated because the stupid cooler was leaking a puddle near my ankles now. I couldn't let the kids slip and fall in this mess. I looked toward the security guard but he was gone. He seemed to be arguing with a mom up front about moving her car.

I looked for a janitor, but no one was around. The school was spotless, clearly someone worked there. I didn't want to risk a kid falling in the puddle I made, so I reached for my phone, determined to call Carter and have him rescue me from the situation I had caused by being cheap and buying a crappy Styrofoam cooler.

Just as I managed to pull my phone from my purse, I heard someone approaching.

"Looks like you've gotten yourself into a little trouble," said a masculine voice.

I looked up with a grateful smile, and my eyes connected with a guy who I could only describe as GQ handsome. He wore just plain jeans and a t-shirt, but somehow it still made him look well put together and classy at the same time. He had dark hair that was cut extremely short. If it weren't for the clothes, I would have assumed that he was military.

He smiled as he approached me and said, "Need some help?"

His eyes were not quite blue, but not green either. They seemed kind of mysterious. I couldn't stop staring at him.

I stuttered, flustered, "I have—ice—"

He looked at me and then looked at the floor. "Looks like your ice is melting."

I looked down at the puddle getting bigger around my ankles. "Yeah, this cooler sucks."

He positioned his hand under it, feeling around for a hole. His hand brushed mine, and my pulse quickened. I pulled away from him, startled and took a step backward.

Apparently, that's all I needed to throw myself off balance and the next thing I knew, I was on my butt in the puddle with my skirt around my waist. And the worse part was that I had apparently taken Mr. Handsome down with me. In fact, my knee was positioned across his thigh near his crotch and as he picked himself up, I might have brushed against it.

I immediately started having dirty thoughts. He seemed um… well-endowed. What was wrong with me? I was at a school for goodness sake. The last thing I needed to be thinking about was Mr. Handsome's crotch.

He reached down and helped me up, and I hastily

tried to pull my skirt down. I hadn't had a bikini wax in ages. I was so embarrassed. Who knows what he saw?

Instantly, I tensed, but forced myself to apologize as I clumsily pulled my skirt down and bent over to pick up the cooler that had been tossed a few feet away and was lying leaking against the wall. I'd made a huge mess. "I'm such a klutz. And to think I was trying to prevent someone from falling and then I was the one to fall."

"And you took me down with you. And flashed your panties. I've always been a fan of women who appreciate lace, so I'm not complaining. And neon pink is your color, by the way."

His comment caught me off-guard, and I was torn between wanting to run away and hide and wanting to roll my eyes. He sounded so nonchalant, and for some reason that bothered me. I felt like he was mocking me.

"Sorry for knocking you over," I managed to say, still unsure of how to respond.

"You didn't knock me over. You grabbed me and pulled me down with you."

I didn't like the accusation in his tone. I immediately straightened up as I grabbed my cooler and glared at him. "I didn't do it on purpose."

"I didn't say you did."

"You implied that I did."

"Nope. Maybe you're just feeling guilty because you know you're not exactly the innocent one here."

"Woah, I didn't know I was on trial."

"No trial. No jury. I'm just stating for the record that you didn't knock me over. You were falling and grabbed hold of me and pulled me down with you."

"That's not what I remember," I didn't know why I didn't just apologize and leave it alone. Wait a minute. I did apologize. He just chose to ignore it. So I was in the right, and he was clearly in the wrong! I didn't normally feel this need to be right, but with this guy, I did. Who did he think he was? Mr. Fantastic? Just because he was hot didn't make him right. That's exactly why I never dated his type. No humility. Or maybe I never dated his type because a guy as hot as the one in front of me giving me a disapproving look never asked me out before. Not that this guy was asking me out. He was actually just looking at me with annoyance, which in turn made me even more annoyed.

"Listen, I'm just trying to help—"

"Trying to help? By commenting on the color and fabric of my panties?" I jabbed him with my finger and immediately recoiled.

"I gave you a compliment," he said, looking sheepish.

I narrowed my eyes. "About my undies!"

"Well, they were hard to miss when your legs were up in the air." He tried to hold back a laugh and failed.

Now I was outraged and embarrassed. He was ruining my day, and it was only getting started.

I titled my chin, hoping to keep a bit of my dignity and said, "I have a party to get to, so if you'll excuse me."

I walked away as cool as I could, knowing that water was dripping down my legs and my skirt had a huge water stain across my tush. And I had a bit of a limp because my knee was a little sore. I awkwardly made my way down the hall with the cooler in my hand.

"Hey, are you really just going to leave me to handle this mess?" the stranger yelled at me.

"Yes, you're a big boy. You handle it," I yelled back as I rounded the corner and made my way to Great Room B. I pushed the door open and was instantly greeted by loud chatter. There was a group of moms happily setting up what looked like a buffet table.

"Hi," said one cheerfully, "are you Piper, Meredith's aunt?"

I smiled and tried to not limp too badly as I neared the crowd of moms who waited for me. I could tell that they were puzzled by my appearance. They were all well put together. They had on leggings with tunics and fancy flats. I was the only one wearing a short skirt and thin t-shirt. I was a mess, and I didn't even have kids to blame.

"I'm Danny Schultz's mom," she said. I reached out to shake Danny Schultz's mom's hand. I guess she didn't have a first name. Or maybe it was a school mom thing to introduce yourself by your kid's name.

I had heard of Danny Schultz—he was Meredith's best friend and sometimes nemesis. They'd been in school together since kindergarten. I'd heard his mom was a bit of a handful too. But so far she seemed to be just sweet and welcoming.

"Umm… how did you know?"

Mrs. Schultz smiled. "Carter told us the twins were sick so you planned to fill in for Dana. So what did you bring?"

"Nothing with nuts, right? Carter did tell you no nuts?" said a mom who looked really intense. Her eyes seemed to bulge as she interrogated me.

I shook my head. "No nuts. Trust me."

She visually relaxed and then narrowed her eyes. "So what did you bring?"

I opened the cooler. "Fruit popsicles. No nuts. No gluten. No dairy." I was so proud of myself.

The other mothers looked unimpressed. The expressions on their faces were clear. I had failed. But I was determined to remain cheerful. "No, ladies, I promise you. Don't look so disappointed. They're great. All natural."

One parent raised her eyebrows. "All natural doesn't mean better for you."

The rest of the moms except for Mrs. Schultz nodded. Instead, Mrs. Schultz came to my rescue. "I'm sure they're fine." She reached into the cooler and began to remove the popsicles. To my horror, they were almost melted.

"They were on ice… I don't understand."

Mrs. Schultz gave me a tight smile. I could tell she was trying to keep things in perspective and not flip out. I hoped the other moms followed her lead. "It's no big deal… I'm sure we can just refreeze them."

I opened my mouth and then closed it again. I could never be a parent. I couldn't even get the snacks to an event safely.

"I'll take them to the teachers' lounge. There's a refrigerator in there," a voice said behind me. I knew exactly who it was without turning around. I rolled my eyes and sighed inwardly.

"I'll do it, just tell me where the lounge is," I said, turning around and facing him.

There was a gasp behind me and it was then that I felt the draft. I didn't know how I'd done it, but I had somehow stuck my skirt into my panties. I reached behind me and quickly fixed my skirt. Now every adult within ten feet of me had seen my goodies. Great. I was making a wonderful impression.

"Anything you say," he said as I turned back to the table, trying to muster a little dignity. I made eye contact with no one. I just pushed the mushy popsicles back into the cooler and marched past the annoying man.

He tried to look contrite, but I wasn't fooled. He was a prick.

"Need some help?" he asked, quickly walking behind me out of Great Room B.

"I don't need your help."

"You sure?"

"Very much so."

"So where's the teachers' lounge then?"

I stopped dead in my tracks. I had no idea where I was going.

"You have no idea where you're going, do you?"

"Are you always such a smart ass?"

"Ouch."

"Just point me in the right direction."

He fought back a smile and pointed in the direction I had just come from. I didn't bother to say thank you as I walked back toward the teachers' lounge and ran smack into Meredith.

"What are you doing here?" she asked, grabbing me around the waist and squeezing me tight.

I groaned, "Ugh, not so tight."

"Sorry," she said with a small grin. I quickly filled her in on the status of her mom and siblings. "Children are so gross. I'm never having any."

"Agreed," I said before I could catch myself. We both looked at each other and laughed.

"I'm just happy to see you. Thanks for coming."

"Not a problem. I'm delighted to help." I looked around, relieved that Mr. Handsome had gone away. "And now I need your help. Can you point me to the teachers' lounge?"

"Right behind you."

I turned around and saw the huge sign on the door that said Teachers' Lounge. If I were a superhero, I would be Captain Obvious.

I found the refrigerator, stuffed my popsicles inside the freezer, and then made my way back to Great Room B with Meredith.

She quickly filled me in on the monologue that she had done for World Theatre Day. I didn't even know what World Theatre Day was. Had that been a thing when I was a kid? When I was a kid there was just Christmas Day or Independence Day; now there was Grilled Cheese Day and National Dog Day? I couldn't keep up. It made me feel old.

As I stood chatting with Meredith, other kids began to appear. Mrs. Schultz called out to me, "Can you go man the dessert station with Ty?"

Ty? Who was Ty? I hoped Ty wasn't that mean mom who had looked at me as if she had wanted to punch me because I'd had the nerve to say "all natural" around her. I groaned inwardly when I turned to look for the dessert table and saw Mr. Handsome standing there. He gave me a small wave and a knowing smile. He was so cocky. God, he got on my nerves.

"Should I go get the popsicles? They might be at least a little frozen by now?"

"Um, I don't think so," Mrs. Schultz cut in quickly. "We'll just use them next time. Thanks a million. Go help Ty now. Thanks."

She gave me a little shove and I instantly bristled. Gosh, private school moms were aggressive.

Reluctantly I made my way over to Ty and sat down stiffly beside him behind the dessert table that was covered in fruit. There wasn't any ice cream, I noted, feeling a little put out.

I sat there and crossed my arms over my chest. Ty didn't comment. *At least he was smart enough to know when to be quiet,* I thought to myself.

I was very aware of him as he sat there next to me. I nervously patted at my hair and hoped that I wasn't stress sweating. I inconspicuously tried to sniff at my underarms.

"You don't smell."

"What?" I said, trying to stop from turning red in embarrassment.

"I smelled you earlier, and you smell nice."

"Stop smelling me," I said, unsure of what to say. Stop smelling me? God, where was my brain?

He looked at me strangely and then said, "Whatever you say."

We sat there in awkward silence for a full minute before I gave in. I just couldn't do silence. I was a chatterbox.

"So does your kid go here?" I was forcing myself to be nice. After all, I couldn't just sit here for an hour and not talk to the guy, right?

"God, no. I don't have any kids."

"You say that as if kids are gross or something."

"Well, they are."

"Let me guess. Unreformed bachelor?" My tone was accusatory even though I had been guilty of pretty much saying the same thing about kids only minutes ago while talking to Meredith.

"What makes you think I'm not married?" He sounded scandalized, which made me snort with laughter.

"Guys who dress like you normally like to play the field."

"Dress like me? What do you mean? Do you always just jump to conclusions and stereotype people based on how they dress?"

"Well," I challenged him, "tell me I'm wrong."

He shrugged. "I'm not married."

"Ha," I said loudly, feeling vindicated. I felt like I'd won. The other moms shot me a look, and I sheepishly avoided their eyes. Kids were now gathering around our station. Most of them went away disappointed that there wasn't any cake or brownies. Yum, brownies.

"Why are you interested in my marital status?" Ty asked, bringing my attention back to the moment and away from the subject of brownies.

"I'm not."

"Let me guess: you're single."

"But not desperate. So if you're asking me out, you might as well stop now."

He laughed hard, so hard that people looked in our direction.

"What's so funny about asking me out?"

He was still laughing, and I shot him a glare.

"Sorry," he said, trying to contain his laughter. "So let me get this right. You inquire about my marital status, but I'm the one planning to ask you out?"

He was right. I made no sense. This was all his fault. He was too good looking, and I had already embarrassed myself around him too many times to not feel stupid, so in fact, I had instead said something stupid. I was doing great.

I could sit there angry with him or I could change the subject. I decided to just change the subject.

"So what do you do?" he asked me, beating me to the question. I was about to answer, when he added, "I think

I should at least know what you do before I ask you out, or should I leave that question to our first date?"

"Ha. Ha."

He tried to hold back a smile, but he lost. When he smiled, he was even more handsome. I felt so out of my element. I didn't know what I was doing, flirting with a guy like him. Because that was what we were doing—flirting.

I liked the way his full lips tipped up just at the corners when he was trying to smother a smile. For some reason, he reminded of like a young James Bond. Kind of mysterious. Definitely sexy. A little pretentious, but still thrilling to be around. I made myself stop thinking of him that way. I didn't even know him. But I wanted to know him… Which I realized was in direct violation of the contract I had signed with Infinity Connections.

I hadn't thought of it at the time, since I was sure I wouldn't meet anyone else until I was eighty. I had signed a contract to only go out with the guys of their choosing until my membership expired. In fact, I was required to go on four dates, just to step out of my comfort zone. At least, that's what Sylvia had said.

But I was getting ahead of myself. We were just chatting. Flirting. Whatever you called it.

"I run a translation service."

He looked impressed. "What languages do you speak?"

"French, Portuguese, and Spanish."

"Wow. Did you speak all those in your home or—"

I laughed. "Oh please, as my dad called it, we only spoke 'American' at home. I spent some time abroad in South America, and languages come easy to me. So learning French wasn't a big deal. My specialty is Spanish and Portuguese though. I learned French just to make sure I'm not insulted in French next time I go to Paris."

"I've never been to Paris. Haven't been much of anywhere outside the States."

I frowned. Mr. GQ wasn't a jetsetter, breaking hearts across the world? I was surprised. "Why don't you travel?"

"I spent most of my adult life in school and then building a profitable business, so I just haven't had the time or inclination. I also didn't have a woman with neon pink undies tempting me to run around the world with her."

Oh, he was definitely flirting.

"I didn't say you should go around the world with me, just that you should explore things outside the States. Get outside your comfort zone." Now I was starting to sound like Sylvia.

"Maybe I'll do that. Maybe I'll take your advice."

"It's free. You might as well."

He laughed.

"So why are you here if you're not a parent?"

"I'm Danny Schultz's uncle. Call me Ty. And I didn't catch your name?"

"Piper."

"Cool name. It fits you."

Mrs. Schultz found her way to us and said, "Ty, do me a favor. I have a code red."

I didn't know what code red was, but clearly Ty did. "It was nice meeting you, Piper. Maybe I'll see you around." And with that, he was gone.

I must have looked disappointed because Mrs. Schultz gave me a furtive smile and said, "Don't worry, he'll be back."

"Oh, I'm not worried—I mean—It's fine."

"You like him."

I opened my mouth and closed it.

"Don't worry. He's single. I'll put in a good word for you."

Before I could say anything, she went marching toward another table, and I wanted to call out to her when Meredith appeared next to me. She didn't look so good.

"My stomach hurts."

Uh oh. Stomach flu.

"Let's get you home."

I caught up to Mrs. Schultz. "Sorry to leave like this, but Meredith isn't feeling well."

Mrs. Schultz took one look at Meredith and her eyes widened. "Yikes. Yeah, she needs to go home stat. Feel better, sweetie," she said kindly to Meredith, who looked ready to be sick.

I placed an arm around Meredith's shoulder and led her out. I ran into Ty on the way.

"Leaving your post already? I didn't figure you for a quitter," he joked until he saw Meredith.

"Sick kid, let me get out your way."

"Yeah, sorry to ditch you."

"No problem," he said, and I hurriedly rushed past him. I had to get Meredith home. But as I loaded her into the car, I couldn't help but look back at the school and wonder if I would see Ty again.

5

"Goooooood morning," said the voice on the other end of the phone.

I didn't know who it was because I had answered the phone by knocking it off the nightstand next to me. Somehow it had landed right side up and on speaker.

Good thing I didn't use Skype or FaceTime. I was sure I looked horrendous.

"Who is this?" I said with my eyes still closed.

"Sylvia from Infinity Connections."

"Hey, Sylvia."

"Hi, Piper. You have a match. He's very excited to meet you. Would you be open to meeting him this weekend?"

"This weekend? What day are we on?"

"Wednesday."

"Wednesday?"

"Yes, the day after Tuesday, but before Thursday."

"Wednesday," I repeated to myself.

"Piper, would you like to call me back when you're more awake?"

"No, no," I said, sitting up. I wanted to go on a date. No. I needed to go on a date. After meeting Ty, I had been sort of feeling sorry for myself. A date would get me out of a funk. I was tired of feeling like a reject.

"I'm awake now," I said, clearing my voice and hoping that I sounded convincing. "Can you text me his number?"

"Piper, you know the rules. No contact until date night. No texting. No sexting. No communication at all."

"Jeez, Sylvia. What's with all the rules? I promise I'll be good, and I won't text him a picture of my butt."

She laughed. "That's a relief, but those are our rules."

"They're very arbitrary."

"Well, Piper, think of how many times you've met a guy, started texting, started chatting on Facebook and then he ghosted you."

I winced. Yeah, that had happened more times than I wanted to admit.

"So what's stopping him from ghosting me on the night of our date?"

"A five-hundred-dollar fine."

"Wow… does that apply to me too?"

"Nope, if you cancel, outside of an emergency event, of course, it's a one-hundred-dollar fine. Our studies have found the guys to be more... what's the word? Flaky... so we charge them more to discourage that type of behavior."

"I like how Infinity Connections works. So where's the rendezvous point?" Or is that a secret too? I wanted to add but forced myself not to.

She gave me the name and location of a restaurant.

"Whose idea was the restaurant?"

"His."

"Don't I get a say?"

"I called you first and you didn't answer. He did, sooo…"

"Fine."

"It'll be great. You'll have fun. He's fantastic. Trust me."

"If he's so great, why don't you date him?"

"Piper, trust me—if you screw this up, I will choke you."

I flicked my tongue at her and then realized she couldn't see me. We discussed the details, and I promised to give Sylvia a call if my date was less than stellar.

Suddenly, I was nervous. Yeah, it was a few nights away, but I was nervous. This was going to be my first blind date. Ever.

I flopped back into bed and then forced myself to get up two minutes later. It was already ten o'clock and I couldn't waste the entire morning. I had stayed up late working on something for a client. It had been a rush job, but he had paid me really well for it. I wasn't a fan of rush jobs though. I liked to take my time and give my clients my best work. I used to have a business partner who would help with the expedited jobs, but he had retired and moved to France. He had been such a romantic. If he knew I was using a dating service to find love, he would be appalled. But I think what was more appalling was that I had a date in a few days, but I couldn't stop thinking about the guy I'd met at Meredith's school.

Speaking of Meredith, I had to remind myself that I had to pick her up from school today because Carter was going to a conference and Dana was still feeling like crap. It turned out that Meredith didn't have the stomach flu like the rest of the family. She just had way too much candy and other goodies from her classmates who apparently weren't a huge fan of the snacks their parents planned to give them at the after party, so they had come prepared with their own. I didn't blame them. If I had to choose between chips or strawberries, the winner would always be chips.

I went to get a cup of coffee and spent the rest of the morning working. Before I knew it, it was noon and I was starving. I wanted a slice of pizza but figured that since I was lactose intolerant, pizza wouldn't be the best idea. I knew my body stayed bloaty for days after I ate dairy, and that just wasn't a good look. I planned to wear something form-fitting for my date, and the last thing I needed was to look like I was four months pregnant in a dress. *Unless he was in to that kind of thing,* I thought to myself wryly.

I sat at the coffee shop drinking more coffee and working until it was time to get Meredith. I was still working in the pick-up line while I waited for her to come out. I was also Internet shopping. I was a little bit of a shopaholic which was ironic since I spent years abroad living in conditions that most foreigners would balk at. I guess all the years of living like a pauper made me appreciate discretionary income even more.

I heard a tap at my window and looked up to find Ty there. He smiled at me and then peeked into the car to see what I was looking at.

"Hey," I said, slamming the laptop closed. "Mind your own business."

"I just wanted to say hello. I don't care if you spend all your free time looking at panties online."

I wanted to roll up the window and pretend he wasn't there. Why, oh why, did I continue to embarrass myself around him? Then I stiffened up; it wasn't my fault. It was his. He had the worst timing. *Just play it cool, Piper.*

"I find shopping online convenient."

"Me too. But I go commando, so I don't bother shopping for underwear."

I couldn't help myself. I looked straight at his crotch when he said that. And, of course, he caught me. He gave me a teasing smile, and I hurriedly looked anywhere but directly at him.

"Gotcha," he said. "See you later, Piper."

Without another word, he turned away from me and went to greet his nephew with a high-five. And then like the boys they were, they started to shadow box each other.

"He's a big kid," I said disapprovingly to myself. I shook my head. Now I was turning into a stick-in-the-mud. Since when did I have a problem with someone enjoying himself and being youthful?

Oh yeah, since I decided those were the type of men I would definitely stay away from. After all, hadn't I admired that youthfulness in plenty of my failed relationships? It wasn't that I was becoming unbending and losing my sense of humor; I was just finally being practical about dating and matters of the heart. At least that was what I was telling myself.

Meredith popped up while I was in deep thought and hollered something to Danny before getting in the car.

"Hey, kid," I said as she got in. She smiled up at me and was about to greet me when Danny called out to her and ran over to the car.

He shot me a glance and then said, "Meredith, don't forget to tell your aunt about the party. You know, just in case your mom is sick again; I don't want you to miss it."

He sounded so eager and so in love.

Meredith rolled her eyes. "I told you already. I'll be there."

"Promise?" Danny asked.

"I promise," Meredith mumbled. That was good enough for Danny, it seemed. He promptly jumped in the car with his uncle and they drove off.

I pulled off behind them. "So you're going to a party?"

"Yep, Danny's birthday party. I go every year. I'm not sure why he feels he needs to remind me. That's annoying."

"Boys can be annoying."

"No kidding, but Danny is like over the top annoying. His uncle likes you, by the way," Meredith said, going through her backpack and looking for something. She pulled out a tablet and started playing a game.

I couldn't believe she would drop that news on me and then just start doing something else.

"How do you know he likes me?" I asked, unable to

bear the silence. I needed answers, and I needed them now. My love life depended on it.

"Danny said so."

"Okay." That told me nothing. "How does Danny know?"

"He said his uncle Ty was asking about you."

"Did he say why he was asking about me?"

"Because he thinks you're hot," Meredith said, looking at me like I was stupid.

"Oh."

I drove in silence. Did Ty really think I was hot, or was Danny just exaggerating? I liked to think I was hot, but I felt I was more of a seven on a ten point scale. I had plain brown hair, big blue eyes, and a pretty great smile. I was definitely not average, but not drop-dead gorgeous either. I wouldn't describe myself as hot though… more…

I immediately told the inner monologue running through my head to shut up. If he thought I was hot, then hot I was.

After I dropped Meredith off, I quickly made a run to the store to grab a few things Dana needed. The twins were back to their normal selves, but Dana was a mess. I didn't cook so I went to the Chinese restaurant and bought a huge container of won ton soup for Dana and then stopped at a pizza place and bought two pizzas for the kids.

I was on my way back to the car with two pizzas in my hand when a car honked its horn close to me, and I leapt a little into the air, startled.

"Sorry, didn't mean to scare you," called out the driver. I recognized the voice immediately. It was Ty.

"Craving pizza tonight or something?" he asked as he parked his car next to mine and got out.

"For Meredith and the twins."

"You do a lot for her."

"Well, she is my niece."

"Family oriented, that's a nice quality to have."

"Well, if you don't have family then what's left?"

He positioned his back against his car and crossed his arms over his wide chest. Now why in the world did he do that? His arms muscles bulged against the fabric of his thin shirt. He was wearing a white shirt with gray cargo shorts. He looked really, really good.

I licked my lips, and his eyes followed the movement. For a moment, we were both guilty of exchanging a heated glance.

"I would like to go back to where we left off the other day. You know, when you were asking me to ask you out?"

A smirk formed on my face. "You wanted to ask me out. I never prompted you to."

"True. So how's Friday?"

I opened my mouth to say sure when I realized that

not only did I not really know this guy, but I was also bound by my contract to not date him. This was hard for me. I didn't want to break a rule, but how would they find out? Right?

I opened my mouth to say yes and then closed it again. Ty was hot. And a jokester and the type of guy who didn't seem to do the whole long-term thing. I knew how our story would end, with me feeling inadequate and him feeling like a stud because he so easily got me.

I was a grown up now. Or at least, a more mature version of myself. It was time to try something different.

"Ty, I would love to, but I already have plans. Tell Danny I said hello." And with that, I walked away. He was persistent though.

"How's Saturday then?"

I turned back toward him, "I already told you. I have plans."

"For the whole weekend?"

I hesitated, and he knew I was trying to make up a lie. "Come on," he said with a sexy smile. "You know you want to go out with me. Say yes."

"No."

"You scared or something?"

"Of you? Ha."

"Then go out with me."

"I can't."

"You already have a boyfriend? If so, dump him. I can treat you better than he can."

I laughed. "Aren't those song lyrics?"

"Yep, but they're true."

"You're arrogant."

"Nope. Just a little cocky."

We both smiled at each other ,and I could feel my defenses breaking down.

"Okay," I found myself saying. "I'll go out with you, but you better be on your best behavior."

He pulled my phone from my hand, programmed his number in, and said, "We both know that you don't want me to be on my best behavior because that wouldn't be very much fun."

"Define fun."

"You, me, naked; maybe drinks?"

I opened my mouth, scandalized. Although I had images of Ty licking tequila from my belly button suddenly.

"I'm joking. I can be a gentleman… if you want me to be."

His words were so suggestive. He was cocky. And sexy. And funny. And too perfect for me.

He bid me farewell and made his way to the pizza shop. I tossed the pizzas in the front seat and then left well enough alone.

Now I had two dates lined up for the weekend. I was on fire.

"What do you think? Do you think this dress makes my breasts look like a uni-breast?"

"Uni-breast?" I said, half turning around in Becca's direction. She was trying her best to maneuver her body into a super tiny dress. Finally, it was up and over her head. Her long, curly blonde hair had kept getting caught in the straps of the dress.

"I hate when uni-breast happens," she said as she reached into her bra and adjusted her boobs. I did the same, but of course, it didn't have the same effect. Becca was chesty and perky. I wasn't flat-chested, but without a good bra, my boobs tended to prefer being droopy.

Becca had offered to come over and help me find something to wear for my date with Jean-Bernard, the guy the dating agency had set me up with. I was a ball of nerves, but I was feeling better now that Becca was there.

Becca was my brother's second ex-wife, and I thought it was hilarious how I was best of friends with both of his exes. He picked great women to marry, too bad he was such an ass and couldn't keep them. I wasn't sure if Becca had even been married to him for a year before she walked out on him. Rightfully so.

In true Becca fashion, she couldn't spend a moment in my closet without feeling the need to try something on. So the evening went from her coming over to help me find something sexy to wear on my date, to Becca completely forgetting about our mission and looking at herself in the mirror.

I shrugged as I looked at the dress I had on. I guess it was appropriate? Maybe? I didn't know. I felt the agency would probably prefer if I looked classy instead of slutty. I think the dress I had on now would probably be considered a little on the slutty side. It was short, red, and showed cleavage. Becca said it was hot. She was right. It was hot, but it was way too much.

I OPENED my closet again and listlessly started pulling clothes out. I wasn't excited about dinner with Jean-Bernard. I knew he was French, but just his name alone sounded pretentious. If it weren't for my contract, I would have texted him that I couldn't make it. Not that I even had his number. But I read all the by-lines of my contract, and there was no way I was going to cancel this date and pay a $100 fine like Sylvia had mentioned.

IT FELT weird to be pursued by two guys at a time. Not that I was actually being pursued, but still… I smiled at the thought of Ty. We'd had fun during our brief inter-actions with each other. I would never tell him that, but it was true. I didn't know what it was about him that drove me crazy. I guess now that I decided to act like a "grown up" I just couldn't be bothered with men who acted like children. It kind of made me feel like a fraud. But I wasn't in the mood to focus on my feelings. That sounded much too complicated and exhausting. Instead, I would focus on my date with Ty. Ooops, I meant Jean-Bernard. Ty was tomorrow... not that I was counting down the hours until I saw him or anything like that. *I totally was.*

Shoving thoughts of Ty out of my head, I reached for my most *serious* dress. It was a long maxi dress with a deep V-cut in the back that almost went down to my waist. It looked demure from the front and when I turned around it was va-va-voom. I smiled and then my smile promptly fell. I think va-va-voom was supposed to be reserved for date two.

Didn't Sylvia say something about making a man look forward to something? But what did I care what Sylvia said? She told me that she'd been married to the same guy for like fifteen years which meant she hadn't had a real date in ages.

Either way, I found myself reaching for a demure blue chiffon dress, while storing the black dress in the back of my closet for another time. Maybe the little red dress or the black dress would come out later for date number two with Jean-Bernard if he wasn't a complete jerk. Or a quarter of a jerk.

I looked at the picture of him that Sylvia had sent me. He was a really good looking guy. But I couldn't really believe the pictures. After all, Photoshop was used liberally in this day and age. I'd been guilty of it myself. I erased a blemish or two in my own profile photos.

AFTER JUMPING IN THE SHOWER, I got dressed and Becca wished me luck. I made my way to the restaurant where Jean-Bernard and I were supposed to meet. I hadn't been nervous up until that moment. What if he took one look at me and ran the other way? What if I had Photoshopped a bit too much in my profile and he didn't recognize me?

What if—?

All thoughts of what-ifs went from my mind as I caught sight of him. He was easy to spot. He was the guy stepping out of the Tesla with a smile on his face as he scanned the outside of the restaurant clearly looking for me.

I gulped hard. Maybe this birthday gift would be worth it. Maybe everything would go great. Maybe I would fall in love and live happily ever after with this guy with a fancy car, fancy name, and a GQ kind of style. That's exactly what it was. It looked like he stepped off the cover of a men's magazine. He was dressed stylishly in a dark suit and brown shoes. His hair looked freshly cut, and I liked the long-ish beard he sported. He was kind of sexier than Ty. Kind of. Speaking of Ty, I secretly hoped he wasn't walking by at this very moment since I hadn't exactly cut ties with him as the relationship advisor had requested. Yeah, yeah, I was violating the contract, but whatever. It didn't count unless I was caught, right?

"Piper?" Jean-Bernard said, coming to stand in front of me.

I nodded, suddenly tongue-tied. He looked nice, smelled nice. He was probably a bit more than my senses could take.

"How do you do? You must be Jean-Bernard," I said, trying to sound as fancy as he looked. I felt so stupid. Who said "How do you do?" anymore? Grandmas who grew up back in the Great Depression. That was who. To me, I sounded stuffy and ridiculous. I wanted to kick myself.

He didn't seem to notice my antiquated vocabulary. Instead, he smiled widely and I was like... woah. Dude was even more gorgeous when he turned the full force of his pearly whites on me.

"You're even more beautiful in person than in your pictures," he said without a hint of a French accent.

"Thank you." I knew I was blushing, and I knew now was my chance to say something clever and flirtatious, but I couldn't come up with anything. So instead I said, "Are you hungry?"

God, I was such a great conversationalist. Not!

"I'm starving, absolutely ravished." He let his eyes travel over me as he said the last part. Apparently, food wasn't the only thing Jean-Bernard wanted to ravage. Again, I knew that I was blushing, but I was thankful for the nighttime sky I was sure disguised it.

He handed his keys to a valet who looked pretty excited about the prospect of parking the Tesla, and then he took my elbow and gestured for me to walk in as the doorman opened the door for us.

Polite. Rich. Gorgeous. Winner, winner.

I continued to be impressed as we made our way to our table, the maître d chatting happily with us about nothing at all. It seemed she knew Jean-Bernard since she asked about his travel plans.

He was polite, but clearly distancing himself as he answered. I didn't think he was being rude. I thought he was just trying to make it clear that tonight he wasn't open to idle chitchat. He pulled my chair out for me, and I sat down and looked around. "Thank you," I murmured, enjoying the ambiance of the restaurant. It was small, intimate. There were probably about ten tables and each already had diners.

"What do you think?" he asked.

I let my eyes travel across the area again and then smiled at him. "It's beautiful and deceptively large. It looks tiny from the outside."

He nodded. "That's true. I like it here. Not too loud. I like to be able to hear myself think and, of course, be able to talk without yelling over other people."

"Isn't that the worst?"

He laughed and sat back. "I once dated a girl who insisted on large athletic events for all our dates."

"Was she a huge sports fan?"

He shook his head. "Honestly, I don't think she could tell the difference between football and soccer, nor did she care. I think she just didn't like having to talk to me one on one."

"So let me get this right—she would make you take her to like a football game and then just completely not know what was going on?"

"Exactly."

"How many times did you go out with her?"

"About six times."

I let out a bark of laughter. "Are you kidding me? After the first time, I would have said, "No, thank you.""

"She was hot. I was young—"

"So her hotness was the only thing that mattered to you at the time?"

He nodded.

I laughed again, feeling refreshed by his honesty.

He visibly relaxed too. "Like I said, I was young. Now I prefer that my dates be not only beautiful, but also women of substance. It seems like the dating service finally got it right. They paired me with you."

I was flattered. He was a smooth one. "So you think I'm beautiful?"

"Without question."

"And you think I'm a 'woman of substance'?"

"Clearly."

"What if I told you that my previous boyfriends were in the entertainment industry?"

He looked amused. "Entertainment industry? Like music performers? Don't all women have a thing for guys in a band?"

It was my turn to smile. "More like I had a thing for guys in the circus. Clowns, magicians, carnies..."

He let out a bark of laughter. "You're kidding me?"

"I wish," I said with a sigh as I rested my chin on my palm. "I date all the wrong guys. Believe it or not, this whole dating package was a gift from my niece because she knows how much of a disaster I am when it comes to guys."

"How old is your niece?"

"I don't even know. Does that make me a horrible person?" He shook his head, but I saw amusement in his eyes. "How old are kids in middle school? At least I think she's in middle school. She could be in her last year of grade school." My ignorance when it came to children was rearing its ugly head again.

He chuckled. "So a child roughly between the ages of eleven to thirteen was critical of your ability to choose your own date?"

"Yep."

"At least you have family who cares. You guys sound close, especially since I'm assuming your sister or brother paid for it and not your niece?"

"You would be surprised. She's very enterprising."

"She must have sold a ton of lemonade."

"We're firm believers in child labor in my family."

He laughed again, and I joined him. It was nice to have someone laugh at my jokes. All the clowns I'd dated in the past had kind of been humorless, which was ironic to me.

"You have a great laugh."

"So do you," I said as we stared at each other.

A waiter came then and dropped off a bottle of wine at our table. We hadn't even ordered it. Which meant he'd planned this in advance. Nice. I'd never dated a man who was so well-prepared.

He poured a glass for me and said, "You're beautiful. You're funny. And you're unique. Why are you unattached? Why aren't you happily married with two-point-five children now?"

I thought about his question as I took a sip of wine. Why wasn't I married? To be honest, I wasn't sure if I actually ever wanted to get married. My parents' marriage had been a joke. My brother's marriages had fallen apart before they had even started. Did I want to get married? Did I want a husband? I didn't know. I didn't know what I wanted. I just knew I didn't want to get to the age seventy and only have five cats for companionship.

I didn't think Jean-Bernard wanted to hear that. I felt that confession would be a mood killer.

So I made something up. "I don't know. I guess I never found the right one. Unlucky, I guess."

He was silent for a second and then said, "Well, maybe your luck is changing." His tone and words held so much promise. Jean-Bernard was definitely smooth. I would have to be careful with him. He was the type of guy a woman fell for and mourned for years if he got away. *A woman slayer,* I thought with a wry smile.

He raised his glass to mine and said, "How about a toast?"

"What would you like to toast to?"

"How about to new ventures."

"Is that what dating is to you? A new venture?"

"What's the saying? Nothing ventured, nothing gained."

"And what do you hope to gain from this date, exactly, Jean-Bernard?"

"I like the way you say my name."

I was flustered. God, he had a great voice. And he was clearly using it to distract me. I knew he was being deliberate by not answering my question. I didn't date many sophisticated men, but that didn't mean I didn't know how. We chatted and ate, and the time flew by quickly. Surprisingly, I had a wonderful evening, and we sealed it with a chaste kiss. He was a gentleman. I definitely wanted to go on date number two with him. After our date, I got in my car and headed home. I wondered how my date with Ty was going to compare with my date with Jean-Bernard. I was looking forward to it.

* * *

AGAINST MY BETTER JUDGEMENT WHEN Ty called me the next morning and told me that he wanted to take me kayaking in the evening, I knew I should have said no. I didn't know how to kayak. But I was feeling bold and confident. I had two hot guys interested in me. Sylvia had already told me that Jean-Bernard raved about me.

We already had plans to catch up with each other again sometime during the week for lunch. He worked downtown and had invited me to stop by his office. I felt that was a little fast, but apparently Jean-Bernard knew what he wanted. He was a decisive man.

But all thoughts of Jean-Bernard drifted away when Ty pulled up to my house. He had the top down on his convertible, and I briefly wondered if my hair would survive the drive.

He hopped out of the car, this time wearing sweat-pants and a sleeveless shirt. I kind of had the feeling that Ty worked out all the time because he was just really well-built. How did he even find the time?

"Hi, beautiful," he said as I headed toward his car. To my surprise, he caught me by my hand.

My body drifted toward him as if it beckoned me there. He slid his hands up my arms, leaving goose bumps in his trail. Then he placed his hands on either side of my cheeks and brought my face to his. His lips settled over mine, softly caressing them, and then he slowly pulled away.

I didn't even know my eyes had closed. The kiss had been brief. Not even a few seconds but it had been enough to whet my appetite. My appetite for Ty.

He let his hands trail down my arms and then took my hands in his and gently kneaded them.

"I figured that we might as well get that out of the way first. That way we don't spend the rest of the night wondering."

"Wondering what exactly?" I said, giving him a pointed look.

"You stare at my lips all the time."

"I do not!"

"You do. If I had a dime for every time I caught you staring at my lips, I would have—"

"Negative ten cents?"

He laughed. "Get in the car, smarty pants."

I smiled at him and slid into the car as he held the door open for me. To my surprise, once I was in the car, he bent down and kissed me again.

"Another one for good measure," he said with a wicked smile.

I couldn't help but smile back. Ty was going to be trouble.

"Have you ever been kayaking before?" he asked as he pulled away from my home. "I love the style of your home, by the way."

I beamed. "Thanks. I did a lot of the renovation work on my own. And yes, I've been kayaking before. With Meredith actually. We were doing an environmental cleanup in a nearby lake and so we took these huge—" I stopped myself. "Actually no, I haven't been kayaking, that was canoeing." Or had we gone kayaking at the lake? I couldn't remember. The lake, Brock, all of that felt like a lifetime ago.

He laughed. "Now I know your memory can't be

trusted."

"You stole two kisses from me, which one of us can't be trusted?"

"You. Because during that second kiss, I know I felt a little tongue action from you." He glanced at me with a mischievous look in his eyes.

I laughed, appreciating his sense of humor. "Your imagination is clearly running away from you."

He shrugged and put his eyes back to the road. "Say what you want, but I know a tongue in my mouth when I feel it."

"Are you sure that it wasn't your own tongue?" I said, holding back a giggle.

"Ha. Ha. Ha," he said dryly. "Now you're a comedian."

I sat there self-satisfied until we pulled up to a lake. To my surprise, there were other cars there.

"Other people do night kayaking?"

"Yeah, it's pretty popular." He looked at me quizzically then. "Don't tell me you thought we were going to be all alone?"

"Well, I—"

"Dating safety 101, Piper: never go out to a place you've never been before with a stranger. Stranger danger and all that."

I wanted to kick him for mocking me.

When we got to the pier, the entire area was lit up with romantic lighting, courtesy of the little lights strung through the trees, and I could see other couples making their way across the large lake that was picturesque with the half crescent moon sitting above it.

"This is beautiful," I said once we were finally on the water.

"Peaceful, right?"

"Definitely," I said, watching little fire-flies dancing in the air. "How did you find this place? Or do you bring all the ladies here?"

He chuckled. "I actually don't date that much. I work a lot."

"What kind of business are you in?"

"I run a small start-up. It's doing really well, but I'm always looking for ways to expand."

"I wish I was more business minded," I said wistfully. My partner had handled all client relations and marketing, so I felt a little bit like I was drowning now that he had retired.

He frowned. "I'm confused. Don't you already have a business? Like a very successful one from what Danny tells me."

"Do you think Danny and Meredith spend all their time talking about us to each other?"

"Yep. I would say sixty-eight percent of their time."

"What an exact number."

"I'm an exact kind of guy."

"What does that even mean?"

"I don't know. Ignore what's coming out of my mouth. It's just nonsensical mush. This is what happens when I date someone that I'm attracted to on more than just one level."

I was surprised by his honesty. So much so that I didn't know what to say.

Instead, I just rowed. From there we didn't talk much. We focused on rowing across the water until we made our way back to the dock. Within walking distance from the dock was a little restaurant, and he took my hand and helped me walk up the steep stairs to the platform where the outdoor restaurant was located.

I could hear laughing and people talking just above us.

This is such a cool little place, I thought as we seated ourselves at a table only illuminated by a lantern.

For a second, I felt as if he had transported me to a Caribbean island. The evening was breezy, and I could smell the water from afar. I looked at Ty and noticed that in the dark, his eyes seemed more mysterious, which made him even sexier to me. Not that he needed any help in the looks department.

He had such a strong face and a confidence about him that I found appealing on so many levels. I had never dated someone like him before. Yeah, he was cocky, handsome and silly, but he also had a quiet strength about him that I liked. For the first time, I was dating a man who I felt I could trust to take care of me. I didn't mean financially. I just meant in general. If things got tough, I felt Ty would be the type of guy to weather the storm without issue. He seemed to be solid.

Sighing internally, I knew choosing between him and Jean-Bernard was going to be tough. It was my own fault. I shouldn't have said yes to Ty, and now I was in a predicament. There were two men in my life who I genuinely liked.

"So tell me about all the places you've traveled." His question was a welcomed distraction from my thoughts.

I began to tell him about my trips throughout South America. He listened, leaning in as if he wanted to know everything. He asked a lot of questions and seemed genuinely interested.

"So why did you come back to the States?"

"I missed home, my friends, and family," I said simply. "Is your family here?"

"No. It's just me."

"No wife and kids sitting around somewhere waiting for you to come home?"

He laughed. "Not that I'm aware of." He stretched his hands out in front of him and took mine. "Now it's my turn to ask: Do you have a husband at home? Watching Netflix by himself, with your toddler on his knee waiting for you to come home?"

The image made me laugh. And when I was done, Ty said, "I love hearing you laugh."

"I laugh a lot when I'm with you."

"I hope that's because I'm funny and not just funny looking."

"A little bit of both," I teased.

He laughed with me then, and I thought again about how easy going he was. My other boyfriends had been so uptight, so sensitive. Ty was a breath of fresh air.

We ordered a couple drinks and a giant plate of nachos and devoured them while talking about nothing in particular. I found out that he was from Washington state. He found out that my brother was a terrible person and was probably on his third or fourth wife somewhere in America or maybe abroad. Who knew?

"Everyone wants to get married," he commented. "But no one wants to put in the effort it takes to make a marriage work."

"I think some people fall in love with the idea of marriage and forget about the sacrifice it takes."

"Hmmm… I would say less sacrifice and more compromise."

I thought about my own parents' dysfunctional relationship but didn't want to ruin the night with their sad story. "I think you're partially right."

"Partially? Like fifty-six percent right?"

"More like forty-five."

"That's mostly wrong then."

"Yay. You know math."

He smiled widely and said, "Now that you've trampled all over my ego, would you like me to take you home? I know it's getting late."

I didn't want the evening to end, but he was right.

Silently, he took my hand again and led me down the steps back to his car. I slid in when he opened the door for me, on high alert, waiting for him to try to kiss me again, but he didn't. The sexual tension between us was evident, but Ty made no move to act on it. Like Jean-Bernard, he was determined to be a gentleman.

I was disappointed. I didn't want a gentleman that night. Or maybe Ty was just a tease.

"You want to come in for a drink?" I asked him when we pulled up in front of my house.

He cut off the engine and turned to me. "Is this the part where you rip off my clothes and have your way with me?"

"Maybe. If you're lucky."

"I have to be honest, I thought that's what we were going to do on date three."

"Suit yourself," I said as I reached for the door handle. "Date three it is."

To my surprise, he didn't try to stop me. He just came around, opened the door for me, and walked me to my door.

"This is where I say goodnight." Was he kidding me? Hadn't this entire night been foreplay? Yep, Ty was a tease.

Feeling dejected and sexually frustrated, I said in a surly voice, "Goodnight."

He smiled and titled my head up to his. "You're upset with me?"

I didn't want to meet his eyes, but he forced me to. "Don't be angry," he said, before he lowered his head back to mine. He kissed me, parting my lips with his own, allowing his tongue to taste me before deepening the kiss by opening my lips wider.

I moaned, and he responded by resting my hips against his own. I could feel his erection pressed against my thigh, and I reached down and pressed my hand against it. His breath caught, and he placed a hand over my own and showed me how he wanted me to grip him, touch him.

I did as he wanted, and he groaned as he pulled his lips away from mine and began kissing my ears, then my neck, and finally my collarbone. The slow methodical kisses were making me wet and finally, when he brought a hand up to touch my breast, I purred his name.

He brought his mouth back to mine then and kissed me gently as he played with my nipple through my top. All I could think of was how good he would feel against me. How warm his naked skin would be on top of mine. How his shaft would feel inside of me. I wanted Ty badly. And just as I was about to voice my need, he abruptly stopped kissing my lips and dropped his hand from my breast. He pressed his forehead against mine and took a shaky breath.

"You're making this very, very hard—"

"No kidding," I said, stroking his member again through his pants.

He laughed. "That's not what I was talking about. All I can think of are your neon pink panties right now."

"I'm wearing black panties tonight. A thong."

He groaned, planted another kiss on my mouth, this one hard, and said, "We'll have to continue this conversation another night. Can I see you again next weekend if not sooner?"

Was he really leaving me hot and bothered?

"Sure," I grumbled.

"I'll call you."

He placed a chaste kiss on my forehead and made his way back to his car. Puzzled, I opened my door, slammed it shut, and flopped down on the couch.

What was that about?

6

"So how was your date?" Dana asked, sitting down across from me. She looked slimmer and strangely refreshed. I was surprised, apparently stomach flu could do wonders. She smiled at me brilliantly. Dana wasn't the type to smile just because.

"What are you smiling about?"

"I have to have a reason to smile?"

"You're not the smiling type."

She narrowed her eyes at me, and I couldn't help but laugh. "You know what I mean."

"Fine. You got me. I'm smiling because after what feels like forever being up to my neck in sick kids, I'm finally feeling better. I'm smiling because I survived what felt like the plague." She then beamed at me. "And I'm ten pounds lighter without having even tried."

"Nice." I knew Dana had struggled to lose weight

after the twins, and she was still carrying around an extra twenty pounds or so. She had tried a ton of diets and always worked out when she could, but the weight was being stubborn. To be honest, the extra weight looked good on her, and it was primarily concentrated in her boobs and hips, but I knew she wanted her pre-twins body back, no matter how impossible that was.

"Exactly. I'm definitely going to order cake for dessert to reward myself for a job well done. I feel like I've had nothing but soup and Gatorade for the past week."

"You deserve cake for surviving that."

"I sure do. What the heck, why not get cake AND ice cream?"

"Wild woman, throwing caution to the wind," I teased.

She kept smiling and dug into the fries the waiter sat in front of us. I'd already ordered the appetizer for us. Dana was my best friend for ages; I knew what she liked. My stomach growled as I visually devoured the fries. They were covered in cheese, salsa, and pico de gallo. I picked up a fork, hoping to eat the fries in a ladylike manner, when Dana simply reached out and stuffed multiple fries in her mouth.

"God," she said between bites, "carbs are so good. So, so good."

I followed her lead and stuffed my face. It was nice to

get out and see her. I'd missed my friend, and I had so much to tell her.

"Dates," I corrected, referring to her question. "Not one but two dates."

She looked impressed. "That dating service is working out, huh?"

I nodded and then added, "Well, one date was with the agency and the other was Danny Schultz's uncle."

"Danny Schultz has an uncle?"

"A very sexy uncle."

Her eyebrows shot up. "How did you meet him?"

"A friend of a friend."

"Carter and I are your only friends, so that means you must have met him at Meredith's school?"

"Hey, stop taking away the mystery. And I have other friends besides you and Carter." At least I thought I did. I couldn't come up with anyone else besides Becca.

"So how was your date with Danny's uncle? And did you get laid?" she asked, helping herself to another fry before taking a sip of the beer she had ordered. It was very clear that it was Carter's night in with the kids.

Dana was a lightweight. I would be in charge of getting her home.

"I didn't sleep with Danny's uncle. His name is Ty, by the way."

"Ty? Ty what?"

I felt like a dirty, dirty girl. I didn't even know his last name.

"Schultz," I said, but I could have been wrong. Dana didn't need to know that.

"That's a nerd's name," she said, making a face.

"Well, for a nerd, he sure can kiss… among other things."

"So you did sleep with him?" She looked so happy about the prospect of me sleeping with Ty. It was as if she was going to high-five me at any moment.

"No, like I said before. The answer is still no."

"Boring."

"Really? You've only had like two sex partners your whole life."

"I know, and that makes me really boring. But I'm not single anymore, so that's acceptable; you, on the other hand, should be sowing your oats."

"No one 'sows their oats' anymore."

She took a big gulp of beer, slammed the bottle down and sighed. "Such a shame. So is he a boxer or a briefs man?"

"I told you, I didn't—"

"Sleep with him. Got it."

"But I wanted to."

Dana's smile grew wide like the Joker's and she had a glint in her eyes. "I knew it. I figured Ty Schulz was one sexy ass nerd."

I burst out laughing. "He's far from a nerd. And I think you're already tipsy."

She shrugged. "Maybe."

"Not maybe. Definitely."

"So tell me about your other guy? What's his name?"

"Jean-Bernard."

"Ohhhhhh," she said, exaggerating her vowels. "He sounds like a fancy man."

"He is fancy. Very fancy."

"Is he French or are his parents just pretentious?"

"He is French, but I know nothing about his parents."

"Did you get into his pants at least?"

"Not even close."

She made a face. "Is he unattractive? I didn't pay a fortune for you to go out with anyone but the best looking guys. I told them to pair you with guys who could do their own underwear commercials. You know like, Mark Wahlberg. David Beckham. Sexy men."

"Well, Jean-Bernard is actually very good looking."

"So you're dating two hotties." She high-fived me. "That's what I'm talking about. Maybe you could get the two of them together and you guys could have a Piper sandwich."

"A Piper sandwich?"

"Yep, you in the middle, one hot guy on one side of you and another on the other side."

"That sounds freaky… yet delicious. Sign me up."

We both started laughing. For the first time in a long time, I felt like we were teenagers again. It felt good.

Life had led me and Dana in different directions, and I was so happy that we had still maintained our friendship. It had been tough after she married my brother because we had grown distant. She had been busy trying to be the perfect wife while raising a child. I had been busy traveling the world and learning who I was and what I stood for. It was nice to be back, around the familiar, around friends.

"So who do you like better?"

"Ty is intriguing. I want to get to know him better. In more ways than one." I considered Jean-Bernard. "But the Frenchman represents everything I want in a guy."

"What are you going to do?"

"Date them both and hope for the best. And I have another agency-sponsored date tonight. I'm kind of over it, but I signed a contract, sooo…"

"Girl, enjoy yourself. Don't limit yourself. Do what you want."

"You're right."

"I know. I always am."

I gave her a dubious look, and she laughed. "I'm on my second beer. I'm going to need you to drive me home."

"Sure."

"In that case," she said, gesturing to the waiter. "Can I get another beer please?"

* * *

"WEAR THE RED ONE, seriously; it's so much better than that blue one. You look like a character from Little House on the Prairie in that blue dress."

I frowned and looked at myself in the mirror. "That's kind of harsh, don't you think? I think I look very well put together. Classy and elegant."

From the mirror I could see Becca and Dana look at each other with raised eyebrows. I turned around and faced them. "I saw that."

"Saw what?" Dana said, trying to look innocent.

"That look that you just shot Becca."

"You're imagining things," Dana said, trying to fight back a smile.

I rolled my eyes and chose to ignore them. Dana had invited Becca over to help me choose another hot date outfit. Between Dana being tipsy and Becca texting nonstop, I wasn't getting much reliable feedback.

"Who are you texting, Becca?" Dana finally asked, then her eyes grew wide. "Do you have a boyfriend suddenly? If so, please tell me he's not as old as your ex? Yuck. What a geezer."

Becca looked at me, and we both tried to control a giggle. Dana's ex and Becca's ex were one of the same.

"I'm texting my dad. He's going through a mid-life crisis."

"Poor guy," I said, meaning it. I'd met Becca's father, and he was a genuinely nice guy.

Suddenly Becca stood up and grabbed her purse. "I'm going to stop by his house to check on him. I'll see you guys later. And, oh yeah, I don't know what Little House on the Prairie is, but I do know that you should burn that blue dress you're wearing so you can never wear it again. It's kind of horrible. See ya."

And then she sashayed out the door while my mouth hung open.

Dana let out a little burp that turned into a giggle. "Excuse me. But wow, she's right."

"Fine," I said. Maybe my fashion sense was a little off.

Fifteen minutes later I was dressed in a red snug-fitting mini dress with a halter top neckline. I felt like it was a little much, but my date was taking me to a comedy club, so I figured I would be sitting down most of the time anyway. As long as I didn't do any bending over, the dress would be fine. Carter planned to swing by in a little while to pick up Dana, so everything was all set for tonight.

As I was about to head out, I received a text from Ty.

"What are you doing tonight?" he asked.

I smiled down at the phone. I figured I would hear from him sooner or later; after all, he'd already texted me several times.

I texted back simply. "Heading out. You?"

He texted me back quickly. "Nothing. Just thinking about how you looked in that dress."

I couldn't keep the smile off my face as I thought of that night. It felt like ages ago, and I had even seen Jean-Bernard since then, but Ty had been on my mind the whole time.

My phone beeped again, and I looked down at the message as I got in the car. "Call me when you get a chance."

I made a mental note to do exactly that and then programmed the comedy club's address into my phone's GPS. Twenty minutes away, just as I'd thought.

I quickly made my way there, parked the car, and walked up to the outside of the venue. It was a two-story venue with posters of comedic greats posted across the bottom floor.

I wandered inside, not seeing my date, and took a walk down the long hall looking at the posters that were signed by some of the funniest comedians from the 80's onward. I recognized a few of them, but not others.

"There you are. What happened? Did you get lost?" asked a voice suddenly next to me.

I turned and looked at the man whose voice it was. I

smiled, assuming he was joking, but he didn't smile back.

"I thought we were going to meet in front of the building," he said sounding whiny and demanding. I disliked him instantly.

I studied him briefly. He was wearing expensive designer jeans and a muscle tee. He had on sunglasses even though it was dark inside the building. He looked like a member of a 90s boy band. I guess that look was back in vogue. I would have thought he was cute if it weren't for his tone earlier.

I ignored his rudeness and said, "I figured I would take a look around the inside since you weren't here yet."

"Oh, okay, cool," he said distractedly as he gave my figure a long look. "You look hot. H-O-T, hot."

I didn't understand his need to spell it. After all, we all learned how to spell hot in elementary school, right?

"Um, thanks." I didn't know what else to say. "You look great too."

"Yeah, all the ladies like this look. Makes me look like a celebrity." He gave me a big smile. I didn't know why. And then his smile faded. "God, you need to loosen up some. Don't you have a sense of humor?"

I was taken aback. What was with all the attitude? "I have a sense of humor, but I wasn't aware that you made a joke?"

He chuckled. "Good one."

I was bewildered. The dating agency had totally gotten this one wrong. This guy, Geoff, I think his name was according to what Sylvia had told me, was coming across as a nightmare, and our date hadn't technically even started.

He then boldly placed his hand on my lower back and attempted to usher me down the hall. I maneuvered away from his hand much to his consternation. He didn't say anything, but I could feel the tension now apparent between us.

He grudgingly bought our tickets, not saying a word to me. He was surly, and his demeanor was off-putting. Determined to make the best of it, I told myself that I wouldn't let his bad attitude ruin the evening. And if worst came to worst, I could always just pretend to go to the bathroom and never come back.

With that thought in mind, I made my way to the front of the club while Geoff came in behind me. He sat down across from me and didn't say another word.

I felt so uncomfortable and thought about calling an end to the date right then and there when the waitress popped up next to us. *Oh well,* I thought to myself, *I guess I'll just have to make it through the first ten minutes of our date at least.* The waitress was a busty, pretty girl, and probably all of twenty-years-old; she smiled brightly at me and then Geoff. He gave her a flirtatious smile and the waitress' own smile quickly became constrained.

"So what can I get for you guys?"

"How about a new date?" Geoff had the nerve to say. He began to laugh and the waitress cast a sympathetic look in my direction. I was fuming.

Standing up, I gathered my purse while the waitress looked on like an innocent bystander.

"Where are you going?" Geoff asked, standing up.

"Far away from you. Have a great life."

I turned and walked away, and he didn't bother to come after me. *Gosh, he was terrible*, I thought to myself. That had been a record for me. I never had a date that ended in five minutes. I considered myself lucky. Ten minutes with Geoff probably would have had me foaming at the mouth.

I reached for my phone, ready to tell Dana and Becca about my horrible date, when I noticed I had a missed call. It was from Ty.

I called him back immediately and the sound of his voice relaxed me instantly.

"Hey, I didn't expect you to call me back so soon."

"My night didn't go exactly as I expected."

"Sorry to hear that." He sounded distracted but not sorry at all. I wondered then if he knew I had gone on a date with someone else. I didn't know what to say, so I blurted out, "Can I come over?"

A long silence followed my question, and I instantly felt stupid. What if he was seeing someone else too? And I didn't even know his last name. And here I was inviting myself to his home? What was wrong with me?

I couldn't take the silence anymore, so I just started blubbering. "If you're busy, it's fine… It's no big deal. I mean, I did just invite myself over. You probably have plenty to do tonight. It's cool. So it's fine if you don't want me to…" I was droning on and on, and it was like I couldn't stop.

"Are you done?" he asked softly, cutting me off and again the sound of his voice did things to my body that I didn't want to acknowledge. I knew if I looked down right then and there, I would find my nipples poking against my dress.

"I—uhh-yeah—"

"Great, then yes, I would love for you to stop by. I'll text you my address. Come right over."

He hung up then without another word and I could feel myself already growing excited as I used GPS to figure out exactly how far I was from his part of town. It turned out that I was thirty minutes away which meant he lived outside of town.

I sped there. And before I knew it, I was on the outskirts of the city and approaching an unincorporated part of town. I quickly found Ty's neighborhood. He lived in a high-rise that overlooked a lake. It was a breathtaking view. I couldn't help staring at it as I parked my car and called him.

"I'm here," I said after he picked up on the first ring.

"Be right there."

I slid out of the car and only then did I realize I still had on my date night attire. I hoped he would just think my choice of clothing was for him. I hoped he wouldn't get suspicious.

I closed my door and leaned against the car. For some reason, I was nervous. And excited. I couldn't remember feeling this way about someone in a very long time.

I watched him exit the elevator positioned near the front lobby of his building. He wasn't wearing any shoes was the first thing I noticed. He was dressed casually in low-slung jeans and a t-shirt that did not disguise the fact that Ty's body was "movie star" hot.

"Hi," I said, feeling sort of breathless.

He stopped right in front of me and gave me a slow smile. "Where's the rest of your dress?"

I laughed. "Are you complaining?"

"No…" He pulled me toward him and slowly spun me around. "You look beautiful in that dress. I'm not sure if I'll be able to control myself."

I gave him a smile over my shoulder and said flirta-tiously, "Then don't."

Together, we made our way into the lobby of his

building and I followed him silently, checking out his backside as he moved in front of me. He then turned around, took my hand in his, and the gentle gesture only served to turn me on even more.

The sexual tension between us lingered in the air. As he held my hand, I could feel my skin heating up. I was already growing wet. I wanted him badly.

Ty was calm and collected. His voice gave nothing away nor did his body language. He led me to the elevator, and it opened for us just mere seconds later.

I tried to play it cool as I rested against the clear glass and watched Ty watching me. I wondered if he could see in my eyes how much I desired him. He leaned against the elevator doors and said, "So did you have some sort of party to go to tonight?"

I blinked, not understanding what he was talking about. And then I remembered his comment from earlier about my dress.

"Something like that," I said barely above a whisper. My date with that guy whose name I suddenly couldn't remember was the furthest thing from my mind. All I could think about was Ty.

He kept his eyes trained on mine as he waited for me to say more. Even his gaze was sexy.

"So that's it?" he said softly as the elevator came to a stop. "You're not going to elaborate?"

"Does it matter? I'm here now."

He seemed to find my answer to be enough, I guess, because he took my hand again and led me out the elevator toward the hall that I assumed led to his place. It was swanky that was for sure, but I barely paid attention to the aesthetics of his building. His warm hand stroked mine and triggered little goose bumps on my flesh. He turned around and looked at me, and I could see the heat in his eyes. He felt the same way, I realized, but he was much better at controlling himself than I was.

Finally, we arrived at his door and he opened it. It was dark, but as we walked further in, our arrival triggered the lights to come on.

I followed him into the kitchen and sat down on the barstool across from him. He opened the refrigerator. "Would you like a drink?"

"I'll take a beer," I said.

He opened one and handed it to me. And then my stomach growled. I was instantly embarrassed, but he laughed it off. "Hungry?"

"Just a little bit."

Food was the last thing on my mind, but I should probably eat something, I said to myself.

"I don't have much of anything," he said, looking in his refrigerator. "Just a bunch of fruit."

"Fruit?"

"I've been on a health kick lately. I eat too many burgers."

"I guess I'll take whatever you have."

He started pulling out fresh fruit like strawberries and grapes. I immediately reached for some strawberries when he said, "Oh yeah, I have cool whip. Would you like some?"

"Sure," I said with a shrug.

I took a moment to look around his apartment as I chewed slowly on a strawberry. It was spacious, but warm and welcoming. It wasn't what I expected from a bachelor.

"So is this an apartment or condo?"

"Condo."

"It's nice."

"Thanks," he said.

"Did you decorate it yourself?"

"Yeah, with some help from my assistant." He seemed like he was about to say more, but then he reached for a strawberry instead.

I shrugged it off and continued to look around. I spied a pile of papers and a laptop open on a table. Clearly, he had been working. I kind of felt bad. Kind of.

"What do you do for a living exactly? You said you run a start-up."

He popped a grape in his mouth and thoughtfully chewed. I tried not to look at his lips, but I couldn't help myself. I couldn't even watch him chew without getting turned on. I was a mess.

"It's similar to a consulting firm."

"Really? And you consult on what, exactly?"

He seemed to carefully consider his response. "Human relations, I guess you could say."

"Hmm, I figured you would be more into the sales and marketing side of things."

"That's definitely not my forte."

"Hmmm… then what is?"

"Come here and I'll show you."

I looked up from the strawberry I was chewing and finished it slowly.

For some reason, it was like I was frozen in that spot. I couldn't move now that I had an open invitation. "Show me what?" I said.

He motioned for me to come sit next to him, and I rose slowly and slid on the barstool next to him.

"So what are you good at?"

He leaned toward me and I leaned in too, knowing that this was the moment. Finally. But I was wrong. He reached right past me, took a strawberry off my plate, and grabbed a little knife. And then, to my surprise, he carved the strawberry into the shape of a flower.

"Where did you learn to do that?" I was impressed. It was something I'd seen on the cooking channel, but I'd never seen anyone do it in real life.

"I worked as a line cook while in college, so I picked up a few things from the chefs."

"The only useful thing I learned outside the classroom in college was how to chug a beer."

He looked pointedly at the beer I was holding. "I guess that's a skill you lost in your youth."

My lips curled in a smile. "Are you calling me old?"

"I'm not walking into that trap," he said, returning my smile. He took the strawberry-turned-flower and rubbed it in cool whip and then said to me, "Open up."

I leaned forward, doing as he said. And that was when he slipped the strawberry in my mouth. It was small, and I took a little bite that was mostly cool whip.

My mouth brushed against his fingers, and we both stopped to stare at each other as I slowly chewed. He brought a hand up and slowly wrapped it around the nape of my neck.

He pulled me toward him, saying, "Come here, you missed a spot."

He kissed the side of my lips, and I gasped when I felt the tip of his tongue.

His hands slowly went up my thighs as he continued kissing me. I parted my legs and gasped as his hand rubbed against my panties. I knew he could feel my wetness through the fabric, and I waited, anticipating the moment his hand pushed my panties aside and his fingers penetrated my wetness.

"Let's get this off you," he said, pulling at my dress. He was quick, bringing my dress up in one smooth motion, and then he tossed it on the floor.

It was cold suddenly, and I realized I was the only person half-dressed. Now that wasn't fair. I reached for his shirt and quickly tossed it to the floor next to my dress. He stood up and let me unzip his pants. As I did, I rubbed against the fullness of his shaft. I wanted to taste him. I wanted to feel the weight of him inside my mouth. I had a lot of wants, but more than anything I wanted him inside me.

He pushed his pants down his legs and stepped out of them. He stood there in his boxer briefs, and I swallowed hard. Yeah, I needed this man, not wanted, but needed him inside me.

He led me to his bedroom, where the lighting was low and his king-size bed covered with pillows looked very welcoming.

But first I needed to know one thing. "Before we go any further," I said as he freed my breasts from the constraints of my bra, "what's your last name?"

He began to fondle my breasts, and I almost forgot that I had asked a question.

"Rylan," he said.

"And Ty is short for?" Now he was pushing my panties down my legs.

"Tyrus."

"So you're Tyrus Rylan?" I said as he gently pushed me on top of his bed, rid himself of his underwear and settled in his bed next to me. He reached for a condom and quickly sheathed himself.

"Yep."

"Nice to meet you."

He laughed, rolled on top of me, and spread my thighs open. "The pleasure's all mine," he breathed as he slid into me.

He met resistance at first because he was so large and thick. I tensed up immediately, and he helped me relax by planting kisses wherever my skin was exposed.

He stretched me with his erection, gliding in and out of me. I moaned his name and gripped him hard as my core shivered around his thickness. He didn't make a sound, while I couldn't stop screaming and moaning in pleasure. I was a wailing banshee while he was still in control. And with each of his thrusts he pushed me across his sheets. Finally, I wrapped my hands around the spindles of the headboard, but I needn't have bothered. He was tired of that position and without any warning, he pulled out of me and flipped me over.

He pounded into me from behind. I met each of his thrusts happily as I rose up on my knees, while still holding on to the headboard. I could feel him opening me, his hands spreading my cheeks. There was something primitive about being taken this way, from behind in wild abandon.

I knew I was about to come. I felt his hand in-between my legs then, playing with my clit as he slowly pressed into me.

"Ty," I gasped as I pushed my hips back and spread my legs more to accommodate his girth.

He continued to play with my clit, and I screamed his name. Waves of pleasure grabbed and entangled me as I struggled to breathe in the wake of my orgasm.

And then to my surprise, he pulled out of me again. This time, he laid down next to me and pulled me on top of him, positioning my sex right above his mouth. I couldn't breathe or think as he penetrated me with his tongue, wrapping a hand around each thigh as he sucked and licked my folds. I rode his tongue, coming again, my wetness brushing against his mouth with every rock of my hips.

The pleasure was intense, but I wanted more, and I began to stroke my nipples as he continued tracing my folds with his tongue, sucking at my juices as I rode his mouth.

I screamed then, and my body tensed as an orgasm of a magnitude I'd never felt before shook my entire body.

My thighs were shaky as I lifted myself off him. I sat

limply next to him, my back against the headboard, and noticed that he was still hard and thick.

"You didn't come," I said in surprise.

I didn't wait for him to answer as I bent down, rid him of the condom and took him into my mouth. I tried to pull him inside completely, but he was too big, too thick. He was delicious though, just as I had imagined. I licked and sucked the tip of his dick, licking off the drop of desire that appeared there. He moaned and thrust his hips up. I couldn't believe it, but I was getting turned on again. I spread his legs and began to play with his balls, squeezing them gently as I licked his shaft from the tip to the base, tracing those little veins with my tongue.

He hardened as I sucked him into my mouth again, and I knew he was about to come. I let my wet mouth slide up and down his shaft going faster. And then he reached a hand down and gripped my hair, gently, not hurting me, but not allowing my head to move either. He controlled my movements, making me swallow more of him as I sucked him hard.

He abruptly pulled my mouth off him and I watched him come, feeling like a warrior princess.

He was still breathing hard as I snuggled next to him. My legs felt like spaghetti, and I was worn out. My eyes closed, even though I tried to will myself to stay awake. I placed my head on his shoulder and fought sleep. I felt kind of unsure now. I had just had sex with him, but I didn't really know him. What was I supposed to say? Did I stick around? Was I expected to leave? I was feeling very much out of my element. Obviously, this wasn't one of those situations where I was supposed to skulk away, right?

"Tell me more about yourself, Ty," I said sleepily. I didn't know what to do next, but I thought it would be a little presumptuous just to take over his bed without at least talking to him.

"What do you want to know?" he said, pulling me closer and lazily stroking my arm.

I didn't know where to start, so I went with my first pressing question. "Why did you let things pitter out at my door the other night?"

"Hmmm…" he said thoughtfully, rubbing a hand down my hip. "I don't take intimacy lightly."

I sat up on my elbow. Now I was awake. "Explain."

"Nothing to explain," he said. "I'm just careful about who I sleep with."

"That's like the opposite of most men."

He shrugged in the darkness and then said, "I guess you're right."

"You could have fooled me. You come across as some sort of playboy womanizer."

"Nope. I'm just a tease."

I smiled in the darkness, and he leaned over and kissed my nose. It was sweet, endearing even. And I felt a stirring that had nothing to do with what was going on between my legs and everything to do with what was going on in my heart. Uh-oh. I was falling for him.

I laid back down and snuggled closer, wanting the intimacy of being held in his arms. He happily wrapped his arms around me and pulled me close.

He kissed my forehead then and I traced a hand down his face, admiring his handsome features in the moonlight. "So let me guess," I said softly, not wanting to deal with my newfound feelings at that moment. "Your parents were high school sweethearts and stayed married for like a hundred years."

He laughed. "I wish that had been the case. My parents couldn't get it together. They were never married but broke up while my mom was still pregnant."

"I'm sorry."

"Don't be. My mom left me to be raised by her parents, but they were just as neglectful as she was, so I ended up living with my dad's parents. I saw my mom randomly over the years and only saw my dad on certain holidays."

"They definitely wouldn't be up for any parents of the year awards."

"Only if they gave awards for the most neglectful parents in history."

"So how was that... being raised by your grand-parents?"

"Probably the best thing that ever happened to me."

"Besides meeting me, you mean."

He laughed. "You think very highly of yourself, don't you, Piper?"

"Only on the weekends when I don't look like a slob."

I could hear the smile in his voice as he said, "I need to stop by randomly while you're working one day and see the real Piper."

"You'll run away screaming."

"That's a risk I'm willing to take."

Even though I could barely see his face in the darkness, I could still hear the smile in his voice.

"But back to your grandparents…"

"Oh yeah, they were great. Very hands-off and provided no guidance, but they loved me unconditionally." He laughed and stroked my hair as he reminisced on his childhood. "They were really permissive. I had ice cream for dinner quite often. They were both university professors who worked until their eighties. I had babysitters from the neighborhood who practically raised me since my grandparents were gone so often."

"Wow."

"Yeah, they were workaholics, but loving, compassionate people."

"So you model your relationships after them?"

"What? No way. Those two argued all the time; I

think that's why they stayed at work so much, to get away from each other."

"That must have been tough."

"Not at all, but it's probably the reason I started studying psychology. I didn't understand why my grandparents stayed with each other when they disagreed over EVERYTHING. I mean, they would be contrary just because. If Granny said the sky was blue, Grandad would contradict her and say it was green."

I laughed. He laughed too and tucked me even closer, resting his chin on my hair. "I guess in retrospect, they are the reason I got a PhD. I didn't understand their motivations at all. I didn't understand why they stayed together for so long but my parents couldn't even make their relationship work for ten seconds. So, in school, I studied relationships—"

"Hold on, so you have a PhD. So you're Dr. Rylan? Did you teach? Were you a professor?"

"I was, but then I opened a private practice and gave up academia."

"And now you're a consultant. And how's that going? Do you like it?"

"Better than I could have expected. I like it a lot."

"Plenty of people have relationship problems… you'll never run out of clients." I tried not to think about if I fell into that category or not. Did I have relationship problems? I had dated guys who had no interest in committing. I'd chosen loser after loser. Yeah, I had relationship problems. But I definitely wasn't going to tell Ty that.

"But enough about me," he said, nuzzling my neck. I instantly felt myself getting turned on again.

He slid down me, planting kisses across my collarbone, on the space between my breasts. Then he was kissing my belly button. I sighed.

He kissed below my belly button and then brought his hands up and spread my thighs. I couldn't think anymore as he settled between them and started to make magic with his tongue.

7

"This goddamn computer is so slow," I said, slamming my hand down on the desk.

"Woah, take it easy," Becca said. She looked at me curiously with her big blue eyes, and I avoided her gaze. She had asked to come over just to hang out, but I wasn't exactly the best company right now.

"What's wrong with you today?"

"Nothing."

"Are you sure?"

"Nothing's wrong with me except that this computer is way too slow."

She said nothing and then turned away from me. "You've been a little cranky all day."

"I'm not cranky. Not at all." Each word was punctuated by me hitting the keyboard as I practically growled at Becca. I was cranky. Yep. But I didn't want to tell

Becca why. I was too embarrassed to tell her anything. I felt like crap, and I didn't want to tell any of my friends the reason I was so pissed was because of a man. I hadn't heard from Ty all week. After the night I showed up at his condo, he had pretty much disappeared from my life. I hadn't received a text, a phone call, just silence. Painful silence. And so I hadn't reached out to him either. I had too much pride to grovel.

The first day I had been fine. By the second day, I had been staring at my phone willing it to vibrate or ring. But nothing. He had manipulated me. Teased me into sleeping with him. He didn't take intimacy lightly, he had said. What a joke. He was exactly who I thought he had been: a playboy, a womanizer. And he had gotten me exactly where he wanted. He had known what he was doing when he had left me wanting him that night on my front porch. He had known that his decision to not sleep with me that night had whet my appetite for him. And then he had had his way with me as soon as the opportunity arose. I had made things so easy for him.

I felt like a fool. I was so stupid. I had made another bad choice. I wanted to cry, but I wasn't going to. I would be strong and just move on. After all, wasn't that what I always did? My love life was like a broken record stuck on repeat. I was tired of feeling this way, but I didn't know what to do about it.

"I'm fine, just sleepy."

"If you say so… So are you seeing someone this week? Another hot date?"

I shrugged. "Maybe. Don't know." I knew Becca was just trying to make conversation, but I didn't feel like talking. I was too busy feeling sorry for myself.

"Just call him."

"Call who?"

"Whoever you're so gaga over."

"I'm not gaga over anyone."

"Then why do you keep staring at your phone, willing it to ring?"

I refused to acknowledge what she'd said. "I'm fine. I think I'll just head out for a walk." I stood up and glanced at my phone.

I was determined to leave my phone there, but I couldn't help myself. I grabbed it and stuck it in my pocket. I ignored Becca's pointed look.

"What?"

"Nothing."

But I heard a laugh as soon as I walked out the door. Great. Now she was laughing at me.

My phone rang, and my heart skipped a beat. I rushed to retrieve it from my pocket and put it up to my ear. "Hi," I said breathlessly without looking at the caller ID.

"Hi, Piper, this is Sylvia."

I tried to hide my disappointment as I said, "Hi, Sylvia."

"Everything okay? That was the most unenthusiastic greeting I've gotten in a long time. I hope you're not still angry about your date with Geoff? Again, I apologize that you were somehow paired with him. I'm not sure how that happened. Our system is flawless."

"Apparently not…"

She had called me the day after my date with Geoff to apologize. Apparently, he had been a big baby and had complained about my disappearance to the agency. Sylvia had been totally on my side. She was a sweetheart. I just didn't feel like talking to her now. There was one person I wanted to talk to, and that person clearly didn't want to talk to me.

"So, as you know, Jean-Bernard really wants to see you again. It's just that he's been out of the country working."

I grunted in reply. I hadn't thought of Jean-Bernard in awhile, but maybe he could help distract me from this whole Ty disaster. Jean-Bernard had texted me recently and I had responded, but I couldn't remember what he had texted me about since my mind had been occupied by Ty.

Ty. What a waste of my time and energy.

I realized then that Sylvia was waiting for me to use

words instead of grunts. I sighed. "Yes, I know he'd like to see me again."

"Would you be open to another date with him?"

"Yeah. I have nothing better to do," I grumbled.

"Okkkkkay then," Sylvia said, clearly taken aback by my response, but not wanting to press her luck further. "You know, you can choose to try a different match, if you like."

"Really? I thought I had met my quota already?" How many guys had I dated? There was Jean-Bernard, Geoff…and Ty. But Ty wasn't associated with the agency.

"No, not at all. Plus Geoff was a dud, so we would like to make that up to you."

"Hmm… you know what? Why not?" I found myself saying. I needed a distraction from Ty and I needed one now.

"Great. I'll send you details."

I made a noncommittal noise, thanked her for her time, and hung up.

Great, I'm going on another date. Woohoo, I said to myself. Becca was right. I was cranky, and clearly I didn't know what I wanted. Actually, I did know what… or rather, *who*, I wanted. He just didn't want me.

* * *

THE NIGHT OF MY DATE, I pulled my hair into a tight bun and put on a black silk jumpsuit and dangly earrings. I added dark red lipstick and a little eyeliner and looked at myself in the mirror. I looked beautiful, but kind of unapproachable. *Good,* I thought to myself. That was exactly the look I was aiming for. I was feeling pretty crappy about myself, but I wasn't going to let my inner turmoil be reflected on the outside. I still needed to look hot, no matter how messed up I felt on the inside.

I got in my car and gingerly made my way downtown. I wasn't looking forward to my date, so I took my time getting there. Truth be told, I wasn't excited at all. I had been tempted to call Sylvia and cancel, but part of me knew the best way to get over one guy was to date another. I knew I couldn't just sit in the house and mope. I was a grown woman, not a fifteen-year-old.

As I neared the exit to downtown, I glanced at my GPS wondering which exit led to the museum. That's where my date had decided he wanted to meet. *At least my date was classy,* I thought to myself, trying to have a better attitude about the situation. Ty still hadn't called. I was determined to just not think about him, but I did whenever I let my guard down. I had thrown myself into work and had even started looking into maybe bringing on another partner to do the sales and marketing side of the business. But no matter how much I tried to focus on other things, I just couldn't get Ty out of my head. It infuriated me.

But I was determined to have a good time, Ty be damned. Feeling fancy, I tossed my keys to the valet in front of the museum and hoped that I wouldn't regret that decision later when I had to pay the bill. Sylvia had explained to me that the museum was having a special exhibit so many high-rollers would be attending. That definitely explained why the museum had hired a valet service. And to my surprise, as I walked in, there was an orchestra playing in the lobby and men in tuxedos were serving glasses of champagne.

I was supposed to meet my date in the modern art section of the museum, but I had never visited the museum before, so I didn't know where I was going as I wandered directionless from room to room, unim-pressed. I wasn't a huge fan of art. I knew that made me seem uncultured, but I would rather hang out at the science museum and stare at dinosaur bones than look at paintings of nude women with funny looking babies. Not that I was about to tell my date that.

The event was going really well if you considered how big the crowd was. For the most part, everyone was happily chatting with each other while admiring the art around us. I was clearly the only one not enjoying myself. I looked left, then right, searching for a sign or something that would direct me to the modern art section but I didn't find one. Shrugging to myself, I just continued to walk around figuring that I couldn't miss a section of the museum that was bound to have a bunch of canvases with paint splattered randomly on them.

A smartly-dressed waiter spotted me and made a beeline in my direction. He insisted that I take a glass. "Compliments of the museum," he said when I opened my mouth to refuse. I quickly found myself with champagne in my hand. *My date wasn't here yet,* I thought with a shrug as I took a sip. I was not in a good mood, so that was probably for the best. I was still pissed at Ty. And my thoughts were totally not on my prospective date.

"Fancy meeting you here," came a voice from behind me. My heart quickened, and I turned slowly in its direction.

Ty stood there wearing a suit that made him look powerful and seductive. I couldn't believe he was so good looking and that I had slept with him. I had really hit the jackpot, and then I remembered that he hadn't bothered to call me since the evening we'd spent together.

But I didn't want him to know that his silence had really hurt my feelings. I didn't want him to know that he had the power to hurt me at all.

I tried to keep my voice neutral as I said, "Good evening, Tyrus. How are you?"

"Tyrus? That's a little formal." I said nothing more, so

he continued on with a strangely teasing tone, "So are you here waiting for your date or something?"

How did he know I was seeing other people? I guess it was the most reasonable guess. I felt vindicated. At least he wouldn't think I was stuck on him.

I decided to play it cool. "That's none of your business."

"Ouch. You're awfully testy this evening."

He reached for my hand, and I pulled away. So much for playing it cool. That wasn't going to happen. I was still too angry.

"What are you doing here, Ty?"

He placed his hands in his pocket and studied me, as if trying to figure out what I was thinking.

"Trying to have a nice time with a beautiful woman."

"Really?"

"I understand that you're angry, but I have a perfectly good explanation—"

Explanation? I wanted more than that. I was ready to tell him off, but I kept my anger in check. "If you excuse me, I have a date tonight."

He seemed unperturbed by what I said. So I guess he wasn't the jealous type.

"Date? I don't see a date."

I bit my lip in frustration. Where was my date? "He'll be here soon. Enjoy your evening."

"Piper," he started, but I turned to walk away and was

relieved when he didn't follow me. I had a date to get to; although, it was beginning to look like I had been stood up. Sylvia hadn't had a chance to send me a photo of my date, and I didn't even know his name. She had just told me that he would find me and identify himself as being part of the agency.

I rounded a corner and stopped dead in my tracks, Jean-Bernard sat less than five feet away from me, talking to someone. I knew at any moment he was going to turn around and see me standing there.

I counted down, "One... two... three..." He glanced in my direction and did a double take. He smiled at me, looking surprised yet delighted to see me. He excused himself then and made his way toward me.

I slowly met him halfway. To my surprise, he didn't keep his distance; instead, he reached out and kissed my cheek.

"What a pleasant surprise. If I had known you were into art, I would have invited you to be my date."

I smiled tightly. It was nice to see him, but I was expecting my date at any minute and Ty was here. Things were not going to plan. I didn't want them all to know that I was seeing other people. I was sure Jean-Bernard knew, but this was still super awkward.

Over his shoulder, I could see Ty approaching. Why was I running around and hiding the fact I was dating other people when clearly what had happened between me and Ty had just been a one-night stand? It had meant nothing to him, so it was time that I followed suit. I hooked my arm around Jean-Bernard's and said, "How about you give me a tour?"

He smiled down at me. "How about I introduce you to one of the artists?"

"That would be great."

I didn't bother to search for my date. Clearly, my date wasn't going to show up. Jean-Bernard was here. And I was determined to have a good evening.

An hour later, I sat next to Jean-Bernard as he joked with his friends. His friends were clearly the elite of the city. I had met a high-powered doctor who collected rare artifacts and angered his neighbors by keeping the artifacts on display in his front lawn for people to take pictures of. I had met an actress who had been super popular in the early 2000s and was now a major bene-factor in the arts. And I had met a child prodigy who was renowned the world over for his expertise in microbiology. They were all very nice and genuinely friendly people, but I wanted to get out of there. I wasn't having a good time.

I had spent the better part of my night ignoring Ty. He always seemed to be lurking around, but he hadn't approached me again. When he would come close, I would excuse myself and disappear into the ladies' room until I thought for sure he was gone. And when I wasn't hiding, I was glued to Jean Bernard's side. I felt like a groupie, but I was doing my best just to get through the night and keep my emotions under control. Jean-Bernard was making it easy for me though. He really was a great conversationalist. He was sexy, rich; everything a woman could want. But the truth was, I barely paid any attention to him. I was only sticking to him like glue in order to avoid talking to Ty. I was using him, and I felt terrible about that.

What was wrong with me? Why couldn't I just be an adult and behave like one? Why was I hiding?

"What do you think, Piper?" asked the child prodigy, pulling me away from my thoughts.

"Hmmm?" I said, realizing that all the others were looking at me. Uh-oh. What were we talking about? I thought about bluffing, but I figured I might as well spare myself the humiliation and admit that I hadn't been listening. "I'm sorry, can you repeat what you said? I've had a long day so my attention span is suffering because of it."

He smiled at me kindly and said, "That's okay. I was asking if you think this building is an improvement over the other one. It's beautiful and all, but a lot less intimate than the original design."

I didn't want to admit that I had never visited an art museum in my life, so I said, "This design is beautiful, but I think the space could have been used more creatively to foster a sense of intimacy."

He and the others nodded in agreement, and I sighed under my breath. Great. I had dodged that bullet. And sitting there next to Jean-Bernard and all his friends made me feel like an imposter. This just wasn't me. Even if I hadn't spent the evening dodging Ty, I wouldn't have had a good time no matter how hard I tried. Jean-Bernard's life was probably full of evenings like this. Evenings where I would feel like the odd-man, or odd-woman out because our interests were so different. We were too different. I liked Jean-Bernard, but I didn't think my feelings for him would grow beyond that. It was time to tell Sylvia that things between me and Jean-Bernard were not going to work out. I felt terrible. Jean-Bernard was a nice guy, just apparently not the right one for me. But it would be okay... for him at least. I was sure he would find what he was looking for with someone else. As I thought about how I felt about Ty, I didn't think things would be as simple for me.

I placed a hand over Jean-Bernard's and he stopped mid-conversation and turned to look at me. I gave him a soft smile. "I think I'm going to head out. Want to walk me to my car?"

"Sure," he said. I said my goodbyes to his friends and then stood up.

He took my hand, and I couldn't help but feel terrible

that things hadn't worked out between me and him. As we exited the museum, I noticed the crowd had considerably thinned. I surreptitiously looked around, hoping that Ty had also gone. The last thing I needed was for him to witness me sort-of-kind-of dumping Jean-Bernard.

"Thanks for being my unofficial date for the evening," Jean-Bernard said, taking both my hands and placing a chaste kiss on the back of them. He lowered my hands and smiled at me, before leaning in to kiss me. I pulled away, and he looked at me curiously. "Is something wrong?"

I nodded and looked away, feeling horrible for what I was about to say. "Jean-Bernard, I don't think—I—"

"Shh," he said, letting go of my hands and giving me a regretful smile. "You don't have to say it. I guess we're not a match after all." His voice sounded disappointed, and I instantly felt like crap. I didn't break up with guys. They normally broke up with me. This was new territory.

"It's not that."

He shrugged and gave me another regretful smile as he slowly shook his head. "I just hope you find what you're looking for, Piper. Actually, I just hope you know what you're looking for."

He turned away from me and silently walked away.

Feeling like I was ready to cry, I signaled for the valet to get my car. Within minutes, he pulled up and placed the car in park. I paid the valet, reached for the handle of the door, and paused. I knew what I was waiting for. I was hoping that a certain someone would stop me. That someone was Ty. But he wasn't there. And I figured he probably wouldn't stop me now anyway. I'd made a mess of everything, and I just wanted all my problems to go away.

As I drove home, all I could think of was what Jean-Bernard had said. Maybe he was right. Maybe I didn't know what I wanted. Maybe that was why I chose all the wrong men. Or maybe that was my problem. I always let the man choose me, but I never chose the man. I dated whomever was even remotely interested in me. I gave everyone a chance, especially the low-lifes, the men without real jobs, ambition, or morals, apparently. I always told myself it was because I liked to date men who were unique and thought outside the box, but maybe I just liked dating the rejects because then maybe they wouldn't reject me. I didn't know what my problem was. I just knew I had issues. And maybe I needed to solve them on my own.

The next day, I got a call from Ty. I didn't answer. I had some demons I needed to exorcise and I couldn't do that around him. What Jean-Bernard had said had resonated with me.

I was still lying in bed feeling sorry for myself and thinking of Jean-Bernard's words when Sylvia called. I reluctantly picked up the phone. *If I was determined to change myself, it might as well be now,* I thought sullenly.

"Hi," said Sylvia when I greeted her.

"Hi," I said, and cut straight to the point. "So my date never showed up."

She was silent for a long moment and then said, "That's surprising—I could have sworn—Are you very sure? Maybe you missed him?"

"Nope."

She sighed deeply, and I wondered if she was finally fed up with me and my inability to be happy. I didn't blame her. I was fed up too. "I'm sorry about that. Can you give me a second, please?"

She placed me on hold, and I patiently waited. A few minutes later she came back to the phone and said, "We've authorized for you to go on another date with a totally new—"

"No thanks."

"I'm sorry?"

"Sylvia, I just think it's best if I figure this whole dating thing out on my own. Take a break from dating maybe. You know?" In my voice, I heard defeat. I hoped she didn't hear it too.

"I'm sorry to hear that," she said after a long pause. "I'll be sure to issue you a full refund. And I'm so sorry this didn't work out. I really wish you the best of luck, Piper. You deserve love. Everyone does."

I didn't know why, but I teared up. She was right, I did deserve love. But I had no idea what I was doing or how to find it. To be honest, I didn't even know what it felt like to fall in love. I was at a loss. And now, I wouldn't even have Sylvia to help me.

We said our goodbyes, and I sighed as I sat up in bed. I closed my eyes and tried to clear my thoughts. It wasn't working. I needed to get out and do something. I couldn't just sit there. I stood up, took two steps toward my door and then sat back down. I was still just wearing my pajamas. That was when Dana called. She started talking as soon as I answered. I didn't even get a chance to say hello.

"Hey, do you think you can do a school event with me again? I don't want to be bored out of my mind."

"Sure." I would rather do that than sit at home trying to get my emotions in order. That was going to be way too hard of a task. "When is it and what do I need to do?"

"It's a family fun run."

"Nope. No thank you. I don't want to workout. I just want to sit here and pretend all is right with the world and that I'm not a disaster of a human being."

There was a long silence, and I wanted to pinch myself for revealing so much. I hadn't told Dana yet about my disastrous night.

"Umm... that's pretty harsh. Why are you beating yourself up? Is everything okay?"

I gave a forced laugh. "Everything is great." I paused, trying to come up with something reassuring to say "I'm just a little antsy because I have so much work to get done since I'm now partnerless."

"Well, I only speak one language so I can't help with the translation part of your business, but if you have any projects that I can help you with that don't involve translation, I'd be more than happy to help. I pretty much have gotten the hang of this whole social media thing, so I could help you with social media marketing if you needed."

"That's sweet of you to offer," I said, truly appreciative. "And yeah, I could use some help. How about we talk about it after the fun run?"

"So you'll come?"

"Yes, to be a spectator but nothing else. I'm not running. I'm not even going to walk."

"That's fine. You can just cheer."

"Excellent. I've always wanted to be a cheerleader."

Dana laughed. "You hated cheerleaders."

"That's because they got all the boys. Something I'm

having a very hard time doing..." Oops, I had already said too much.

Dana immediately caught on. "The dating agency isn't working out, huh?"

"I'll tell you all about it later."

We got off the phone, and she texted me the location and time of the event.

I made myself work a little and then I got dressed and headed to the event. It was on school grounds but located about a mile behind the main facility. I parked my car and got out.

As soon as I got out of my car, Meredith was there. "Finally!" she said, clearly exasperated.

I didn't know what I had done wrong, but she looked pretty miffed. "What's up? Am I in trouble?" I said, locking my car door.

She placed her hand on her hips and glared at me. "You were supposed to be here like fifteen minutes ago. Come on," she said, grabbing me and dragging me toward the field.

"What? Huh? Where are we going?"

"We have our event in like one minute or we forfeit."

"Event? What?! No! No one told me about an event. I can't do an event. I'm terribly out of shape, Meredith. I don't even walk to the mailbox."

She powered on, dragging me behind her. I didn't stand a chance. Apparently kids were really strong.

I looked around trying to figure out what was going on. There was a crowd of at least fifty adults and at least 100 kids running around back and forth. It seemed to be ordered chaos. Everyone was clearly having a great time, and some families even had on matching t-shirts. When we passed the refreshment table, I impulsively reached for a cup of some sort of mysterious sports drink and downed it like a tired marathon runner. I figured it couldn't hurt.

When we cleared the refreshment table, I noticed about fifty feet in front of us were a group of adults paired up with kids, standing idly on the field next to a starting line.

Spectators stood on the side, chatting excitedly. I found Dana and Carter there.

"Hey, you finally made it. You better hurry up or you'll forfeit," Carter said, as if I knew what was going on.

"Forfeit? What is everyone talking about?"

Dana shot me a guilty look. "Sorry, once Meredith realized you were coming she insisted on doing this event with you."

"Mom and Carter are kind of slow," she said matter-of-factly.

"I'm SLOWER." But she was done listening and just continued to drag me to the starting line.

"Good luck," Dana and Carter called out. I ignored

the mockery clear in their tones. They knew I hadn't been much of an athlete since like freshman year of college. And even then, I hadn't exactly been a fierce competitor. I tried to get in a competitive mood by bouncing up and down and stretching. I continued my feeble attempt to look athletic by swinging my arms back and forth as if I was getting warmed up. I was just happy that I had worn yoga pants and a t-shirt with sneakers. I had originally debated wearing flip-flops with very short shorts. Glancing toward the spectators again, I wondered where the twins were and then I saw them. They were hitting each other with paper cups at the refreshment table. I held back a smile.

Meredith started stretching so I awkwardly copied her. As I pretended to know what I was doing, I casted a glance at the other parents at the starting line. They were all shapes and sizes and I felt terrible to admit this, but I secretly was happy that I wasn't the only partici-pant who looked awkward and kind of out of shape.

"So what are we doing?"

"Wheelbarrow racing."

"Oh." I hadn't done that since I was like eight. "Sooo... how does that work? Am I holding your legs or are you holding mine?"

She shook her head and gave me a look of disbelief. "You seriously want me to answer that question?"

"We hold their legs while they make their way to the

finish line by walking on their hands," a voice said from behind me. God, could this day get any worse? Where had he come from?

I ignored him. What the hell was Ty doing there? The announcer's voice blasted through the air before I had the chance to say anything. That was sort of a relief.

"Okay, parents, friends, and students. We're ready to start."

We got into position and I tried to ignore Ty who was clearly Danny's partner.

"On your mark, get set, go!"

We got off to a difficult start and I almost tripped over Meredith, but I was determined to beat Ty. I didn't care about everyone else around us. I just wanted to do better than Ty.

We raced clumsily to the finish line and I glanced behind me, smiling widely when I realized he was far behind us. And then just like that, we crossed the finish line. We had lost... miserably, but at least we had beat Ty and Danny. Meredith and I high-fived, and I couldn't help but laugh. I was feeling amazingly better.

"Congratulations," Ty said as Meredith and Danny excitedly talked to each other. "So how've you been?" I ignored him and walked away. He followed me. "Listen, can we just talk?"

"I don't have anything to say to you."

"Really? An apology would be nice."

I turned to him quickly and poked him in the chest. "You want me to apologize to you?"

"Well, you ignored me and left me dateless."

"What are you talking about? What did you expect me to do? Run to you with open arms?"

"I expected you to at least acknowledge me and not spend your entire evening with someone else."

"Acknowledge you?" I scoffed. "Before I saw you at the museum, you hadn't even bothered to even acknowledge my existence since we slept together."

He frowned. "That wasn't some sort of calculated slight... I've just been busy."

"Whatever," I said, walking away from him.

"I'm telling the truth," he said, trailing behind me again. I pointedly walked away from the spectators and the crowd. I didn't want everyone to see me arguing with my reluctant lover. Or ex-lover. I didn't know what Ty was to me.

He continued trying to convince me as he followed me to my car. Once I reached my door, I turned around and confronted him.

"You have some nerve," I growled. "And to think I fell for your 'I don't take intimacy lightly' line. I feel so stupid."

"I didn't lie to you. Especially about that. I don't take intimacy lightly."

"You slept with me and then disappeared."

"I didn't disappear—"

"Oh really?" I said, opening my car door and getting in. I put the key in the ignition and looked back at him. I couldn't read his eyes, but I wish I hadn't looked into them. Their odd color pulled me in, and I could feel my anger fading and my resolve softening.

"I had to take care of some business and then I knew I would see you at the museum opening—"

"What do you mean, you knew you would see me? How?"

"Well," he said with a sheepish shrug, "I was supposed to be your date that night."

I stared at him. But no. That couldn't be. What was he talking about? He couldn't have been my—

"I was your match that night."

"What? What are you talking about?" I didn't know whether to be mortified or relieved. I didn't want him to know that I had been such a disaster at love that I had signed up for a dating agency. But how amazing would it be if he actually were my match?

"You're with Infinity Connections?" Disbelief was still clear in my voice.

"Yep."

"And that's why you showed up at the museum?"

"Yep."

"Sylvia didn't say a word."

He shrugged again. "I asked her not to."

"Oh my god," I said, putting my hand against my forehead in exasperation. "I told Sylvia that you—well, not you, but my date who now I know was you—"

"You're blubbering," he said, leaning his gorgeous body against my car door.

I glared at him. "I told her that you hadn't shown up."

"Ohhh that explains why she gave me the cold shoulder and then yelled at me. That explains a lot now."

I loved Sylvia. "So when did you join Infinity?"

He hesitated and then said simply, "Recently."

"So you were violating the policy too, huh?"

He looked at me curiously. I guess he hadn't read the rules.

"You know.... us seeing each other when we were only supposed to be dating people from Infinity Connections is against company policy."

He shrugged. "Oh yeah, but no one cares."

"Sylvia does."

"Sylvia is a force to be reckoned with."

"Yeah, but she's a bleeding heart romantic under all that toughness."

He nodded in agreement. "That's what makes her the best at her job."

I thought about what she had told me about deserving love. "Yeah, she's really sweet and believes in the company's goals. She wants to help people find their own happily ever after."

"She's a sucker for romance, that's all."

"Sounds like you got a chance to know her well."

He smiled. "You could say that. So can you please go on a date with me or should I ask Sylvia to ask you for me?"

I closed my car door and started the ignition. He looked at me in surprise. It felt good to have the upper hand even if for just a few minutes.

I rolled down the window and he smiled and began to lean toward me. "Tell Sylvia to call me. Bye, Tyrus."

And with that, I drove away. With a smile on my face, I thought to myself, *I guess I wouldn't be needing that refund.*

8

The doorbell rang, and I glanced at myself in the mirror. I hoped my wardrobe looked casual enough. I was wearing jeans and a t-shirt and had decided on no makeup. After all, I didn't want my date to think he was special. The doorbell rang again, and I slowly made my way to my front door.

I opened it and said, "You're late."

"I had to find parking," he said, checking me out before surprising me by bringing me into his arms.

"Hey," I said in false protest. It felt good to be in his arms again. I could smell the hint of his aftershave and the feel of him so close just felt right. I wanted to wrap my arms around him and settle my head against his chest, but I wasn't going to make it that easy for him.

So instead, I slapped at his hand and stepped out of his embrace.

He looked disappointed. "I can't even get a hug?"

"You're still in the doghouse, buddy," I said as I stepped back into the house, and he followed me.

I closed the door behind us and then turned around and marched past him toward my kitchen. "Come on, get to work," I said ,pushing bowls and utensils towards him.

He looked confused. "I thought you were making dinner."

"Then you misheard. Like I told Sylvia—you're making dinner, and I'm watching."

He rolled up his sleeves. "Seems fair."

I smiled. "Of course it does."

I sat down on the couch and started watching TV as I listened to him digging through the refrigerator.

"Are you seriously not even going to help?"

"Nope," I called back contently.

"How about at least pull a chair around and keep me company?"

"No thanks."

"I don't think it's a real date unless you keep my company."

"Then I guess this isn't a real date."

"So what am I? Your personal chef who you just happened to have sex with?"

I knew he was just trying to change the tone of the

evening, but I wasn't going to let him. "Consider that a one-time anomaly."

"So which position was your favorite?"

I could feel my skin growing warm at the reminder of the things we did that night. But I tried to push those thoughts away. Boy, was that hard.

"I refuse to answer that question."

"I would say from behind because you have a great ass, but watching you orgasm... seeing your face... now that was—"

He didn't get another word out since I picked that moment to pick up a throw pillow and toss it at him. And luckily my aim was true.

"Hey," he said, pushing the pillow off the island where it had ended up after it collided with his face. "No pillow fights unless we're in bed."

I changed the channel and looked at him then. He had a stupid smile on his face, and I couldn't help but laugh. "It's nice to have fantasies."

"Ha," he laughed dryly. "So what are you saying?" he asked as he continued chopping vegetables. "You're saying us together in bed again is just a fantasy that won't come true? I don't believe that for a second. And neither do you."

"Whether I believe it or not, that's not going to happen tonight."

He gave me a sad look, and I held back a laugh. "The puppy dog eyes aren't going to convince me otherwise."

He shrugged and started cooking. "It was worth a try."

I settled back in front of the TV and deliberately ignored Ty while he cooked. Yeah, this date had been my idea, but I had been determined to keep some distance... not just physically but emotionally. I didn't completely trust Ty yet. I didn't trust that he wouldn't do another disappearing act and just blame it on work. Even though he was actively trying to find someone, since he had joined the agency and all, that didn't mean he was ready or open to a relationship. And that was what I wanted. A real relationship. I wasn't settling for anything less.

Ten minutes later, he sat down on my couch next to me and stared at the television.

"What are we watching?" he said, trying to snake an arm behind me. I pinched him, and he yelped, "Ouch."

"Keep your hands to yourself."

"I just wanted to hold you."

"Not an option."

"How about your hand? Can I at least hold your hand?"

"No."

"Why not?"

"It's busy holding the remote."

"You're so mean. That tidbit of information wasn't in your eval."

I frowned. "You've seen my evaluation?" How had that happened? I thought only Sylvia had access to the clients' evaluations. And surely, she didn't release that info to prospective dates?

"I'm saying that it must have not been in there; otherwise, you wouldn't have been paired with me, you know, someone so decent and kind."

I narrowed my eyes at him. "Decent and kind? How about conceited and secretive?"

He seemed to think about my description of him and said, "Hmmm... maybe you're right." Then he stood up abruptly. "Dinner's ready."

"That fast?"

He gave me a beautiful smile. "What can I say? I'm gifted at many things, as you know." He gave me a suggestive look, and I rolled my eyes.

"You're ridiculous," I said as he pulled out a dining room chair for me to sit down. As I sat down he scooted my chair in and kissed my cheek. "I am ridiculous, but you love it."

He turned away and finished getting dinner prepared, and I just took that moment to stare at him. My whole body was aware of him. It was like whenever he was around, every cell of my body tensed.

He looked good tonight, wearing just a casual pair of shorts and a plain white tee. That plain white tee didn't disguise the fact that he had great shoulders. I remembered what it felt like that night to wrap my arms around those shoulders. And at that moment, he turned around and sent me a knowing smile. I promptly looked elsewhere. He appeared beside me and started placing plates on the table.

"I saw you checking me out," he said casually.

"I wasn't checking you out."

"Then what would you call it?"

"I was staring, spacing out in boredom, and you happened to be in my line of vision."

"Ouch, are you saying that I'm boring?"

"If the shoe fits…"

He gave a bark of laughter and squeezed my shoulder. I shifted away from his touch. God, even a casual touch from him lit me on fire.

"Oh, I'm sorry… are we still doing that no touching thing?"

"Yep."

"That's a shame. There's so much of you I would like to touch. Or kiss," he said, looking at my lips.

I nervously licked them, and he followed the motion with his eyes. "Stop tempting me."

He turned away, and I fought back a smile. I was glad

my no touching rule was hard for him too. He finished setting the table without another word, and then he sat down across from me.

"So this is the masterpiece I created based on the paltry offerings in your refrigerator."

And he was right, it was a masterpiece. And to think that he had made all of this with some leftover herbs, half a box of pasta, and a few tomatoes.

"This is wow, yeah, a masterpiece. I hope it tastes as good as it looks," I teased.

I helped myself to a plate of it and dug in. "This is delicious. My compliments to the chef."

"Thank you."

"Maybe this can be your fall back career. You know, when you retire."

"I don't plan on retiring."

I looked at him in surprise. "You plan to work the rest of your life?"

He shrugged. "My grandparents did. I figure why not."

"Not me. My partner just retired. He lives somewhere in France now, and he's loving his new life. No obligations, no work. Just freedom."

Ty took a bite and seemed to be in deep thought as he chewed. "I don't know if I could live like that. I need structure. I need to be productive."

I shook my head. "I'm the opposite. I hate structure, and I feel like being productive is overrated."

"Maybe you can teach me your ways, sensei."

"You're mocking me... that's alright; you'll come around to my way of thinking when you're eighty, wrinkled, and still trying to figure out some new version of QuickBooks."

He laughed. "I'll just ask you to figure it out for me."

"What makes you think I'll still be around you when you're eighty?"

"Because I'm irresistible."

"Try again."

"Because I plan to spend the next weeks, months, years, of my life trying to convince you that the only person you want to be with is me?"

I swallowed hard. That wasn't what I had been expecting to hear. I cleared my throat and said nonchalantly, "That type of convincing would take centuries."

"Ouch, you're so harsh."

"Just realistic."

He put down his fork and sat back in his chair. He studied me and said, "All I need is a month."

"A month to do what?" I said, taking another bite.

"To convince you that the person you want to be with is me."

I scoffed. "Good luck."

"I don't need luck. I've gotten this far without it."

"So far the furthest you've gotten is my dining room."

"And my kitchen... and my bedroom."

He let his words linger between us, and he held my eyes. I was the first to look away, feeling naked not only physically but emotionally under his knowing gaze.

We finished dinner but didn't talk much. Or rather, I didn't have much to say. I was deep in thought thinking of what he had proposed. I found his proposition interesting.

"What are you thinking about?" he asked me as he cleared our plates, catching me off-guard. I had been in deep thought until that moment. Thinking about him, actually. Clearly I couldn't stop thinking about him. That was my problem. "Talk to me. Don't leave me guessing or making assumptions."

I wiped my mouth and put down my napkin. "I don't know what you want me to say."

"Say that I still have a shot. I messed up, but it won't happen again. And now I'm trying to make things right." He turned toward me with a dishrag in his hands. *He even made doing the dishes look sexy,* I thought momentarily.

"So what do you say? Can you give me another shot? Give us another shot?"

I had glanced down to think, but I looked up and met

his eyes. I instantly regretted it. His eyes held sincerity. He meant what he was saying. And I felt, deep down, that I could trust him. Or maybe it was just because I wanted to trust him more than anything else. I wanted things to work out between us because I felt that of all the men I'd dated, with Ty, at least I could see a future.

I was going to tell him yes. How could I not? I liked Ty and he was my match according to Infinity, so there must have been something in both of our evaluations that meant we were compatible on some level. We just needed to figure it out and lay down some ground rules.

"Ty, please join me on the couch," I said formally, standing up from my chair and making my way to the couch.

"Uh oh, am I in trouble?" he said as he sat down beside me.

"Maybe," I responded. "If we're going to do this whole dating thing, then there are a few rules that we need to establish first."

He crossed his arms and looked at me with a mixture of intrigue and amusement in his eyes.

"These are the rules," I said, feeling emboldened by having the upper hand. At least, I felt like I had the upper hand.

"Rule number one: complete transparency. For example, if you don't want to do this anymore," I said, gesturing in between us, "just tell me."

"By 'this' you mean have a relationship?"

"Relationship, dating, whatever you want to call it…"

"That rule's useless because I'm not going anywhere—"

I narrowed my eyes at him and said, "Which brings me to rule number two. No more disappearing acts… after we… you know…"

"Tear each other's clothes off again? Get naked? Make passionate, dirty, kinky, love?"

I cleared my throat and glared at him. He had a smug expression on his face, and it took every ounce of my strength to ignore it.

"You know what I'm talking about," I ended up growling.

He tried to look contrite and failed.

"And rule number three, which kind of goes back to rule number one—just be honest with me. If you don't think things are working out between us, tell me. I don't want to be led on anymore or lied to. And if I find out you're lying to me about *anything*, we're through."

"Does this include white lies like, *oh, honey, of course you look good in that dress.*"

I fought back a smile. "That would never be a lie, because I look good in *everything*."

"You're right," he said, leaning his head against the couch and staring at me. His eyes traveled across my face. "You're so beautiful that you could wear a paper bag as a dress, and I would still try to get in your pants."

I rolled my eyes. "You need to work on giving compliments. They start off and then finish terribly."

He shrugged and then caught me off-guard when he reached out and stroked the side of my face. His touch was gentle and strangely reassuring. "I'll stop behaving like a juvenile now and refrain from making sex jokes."

"That's a relief."

He smiled and met my eyes. "You really are beautiful, you know. Ever since the moment you tripped in a puddle of your own doing and fell into my arms, I knew there was something special about you."

I punched him in the shoulder, and he pretended it hurt. He caught my hand and brought it up to his lips. He held my eyes as he kissed it. The simple gesture was sexy in a gallant kind of way. As soon as his lips connected with my skin, that familiar burn of desire caused my skin to flush at his touch.

I pulled my hand away and crossed my arms so I wouldn't be tempted to touch him. "So what do you think of the rules?"

He sighed and sat back. "I think your rules are fair."

"But? I know there's a but coming."

"No buts."

I didn't buy that for a second. But before I could argue with him, he continued talking.

"So do you mind if I watch a little TV with you before I head out?"

I was surprised. That hadn't been how I had expected this conversation to play out.

"Sure. I guess."

He settled back on the couch, kicked his shoes off, and tossed his feet up on the coffee table.

"I'm sure your grandparents taught you better than that," I said, referring to his feet.

"They did, but this is so much more comfortable." He sneakily wrapped an arm around me and pulled me toward him so my head rested on his chest. "And this is even more comfortable."

He kissed my forehead and turned his attention to the game show on the screen. I briefly thought about pulling away, but then thought better of it. I would give in, at least for this one night.

I snuggled against his chest, feeling for a second as if that's where I belonged. I didn't dare let myself think about it further. I was falling for Ty. Or maybe I had already fallen for him, I wasn't sure. But I was determined to just enjoy the moment. I inhaled deeply, enjoying the smell of him, and then I wrapped my arms around his middle.

He kissed my forehead again and then pulled me closer. I looked up at him, trying to ignore the feel of his hard chest beneath my cheek. He was so close. It would be so easy to just reach up and kiss him.

He glanced down at me at that moment, and I expected him to give me a knowing smile or to tease me, but he didn't. Instead, he tilted my chin up and kissed me. The kiss wasn't passionate; it was soft, gentle and when he pulled away, I wanted more. Much more.

But Ty just wrapped me in his arms and turned his attention back to the TV. I sighed against his chest, and he rubbed a hand through my hair and down my back. His hand traced my spine up, down, and then back again.

His touch was hypnotic, and I could feel myself growing sleepy. I yawned and thought to myself that I would close my eyes at least for a little while.

When I stirred again, I found Ty asleep next to me. I didn't know what time it was. I gently extracted myself from his embrace and stared at him. He looked kind of innocent while sleeping, even though I knew the truth. He was anything but innocent, yet our evening had been. I was having contradicting feelings about that.

As if he could feel me staring, his eyes slowly opened.

"Hey," he said.

"Hi," I said back.

He gave me a slow, sleepy smile, and said, "How long was I asleep?"

I shrugged. "Not sure. I fell asleep too..."

He raised one brow questioningly. "Really? Are you sure you didn't take advantage of me while I was sleeping?"

I faked innocence. "I would never do that."

He looked disappointed. "That's too bad."

I laughed then and to my surprise, he pulled me in his lap. He was hard; I could feel his erection pressed against my hip. I couldn't help myself, I pressed against it.

He let his hands trail up my shirt, raising it, and began to gently stroke my back. "I'm trying to be on my best behavior, but you're making this very very difficult."

"Good," I said, wanting him and not afraid of letting him know it.

I repositioned myself in his lap and began to rock my hips against his crotch. His eyes closed for a second, enjoying the feel of my motions, but then his hands stilled my hips.

"Not yet. I made a promise to you, and I intend to keep it."

"I'm pretty sure I didn't make you promise to be celibate."

"I'm not talking about your rules; I'm talking about my own."

He moved to sit up, and I climbed off of him and settled back on the chair and stared at him.

"Care to share those rules with me?"

He began to put his shoes on and then when he was done, he turned to me and said, "No."

I shot him a glance of disbelief and he chuckled, bent down, and kissed me firmly on the mouth. "I'm heading out; thanks for having me over. Come lock the door behind me."

Sheepishly, I followed him to the door trying not to think of how much I wanted him. I couldn't believe he was just going to leave me like this.

He laughed when he saw my face as he prepared to leave.

"Stop pouting," he said, taking my chin in his hand and tilting my face up to his.

"I'm not pouting," I said, still pouting.

"You are. But it's cute." He kissed me again and this time, he deepened the kiss, and I greedily met his tongue.

Abruptly he pulled back, took a deep breath and said, "Have a good night, Piper."

And just like that, he was gone. I closed the door after his car departed and locked it. Ty had practiced great reserve. I wondered what exactly were his rules? I just hoped they didn't include celibacy, because I wanted Ty so bad I needed a hot shower to take the edge off. So with that, I cut off the TV and made my way to the bathroom, thoughts of Ty in my mind.

* * *

"YOU'RE DOING IT ALL WRONG," he said, coming up to stand behind me. "You're supposed to swing from your hips. You're putting too much arm into it. And you're twisting too much."

"Everyone's a critic."

"I'm just trying to help."

"You're just checking out my butt."

"Yes," he admitted with a smile, "I'm doing that too."

I laughed. We were playing golf at the local course near Ty's community. It had been Ty's idea. I secretly thought he just wanted to see me in a little skirt.

I took a swing at the ball, and it went flying through the air and landed about ten feet away. That would have been impressive if I hadn't been aiming for the hole that was literally like a foot away from me.

"Great shot," Ty said, holding back a laugh.

I shook my golf club at him. "You haven't made one shot yet. Like at all."

"That's because I don't want to embarrass you."

"I'm starting to think you don't even know how to play."

He shrugged. "I might have exaggerated my golf playing prowess a little bit."

"A little bit?" I shot him a look.

"Okay. Maybe a lot. I've only played mini-golf. I just wanted to drive the little cart around."

"No wonder all your tips were so horrible. 'Wiggle your hips, Piper.' 'Lean into the shot, Piper.'"

"Hey, that was a good tip. I'm sure all the pros use it."

"And I'm sure that you don't know what you're talking about."

He slung an arm around my shoulder. "Oh ye of little faith..."

I smiled and wrapped an arm around his waist. It felt good to be around him. I was learning so much about him. I didn't know he had such a boyish, playful side, for instance. He always teased me, and it was fun to not take myself so seriously. I realized that I had always been the serious person in my previous relationships. It was nice to participate in the ribbing too. I was actually pretty funny, which was a side of me that normally only my friends saw.

We had been dating for about a month now. And things hadn't heated up in the bedroom at all. Yeah, we had our moments when things came close, but for the most part, Ty planned most of our dates and they normally took place in public outings as if he didn't trust himself to be alone with me.

To be fair, I didn't trust myself to be alone with him. He was too much of a temptation.

He took my hand in his and said, "There's a play at

the outdoor theatre today… it's starting in like an hour. You want to check it out or did you need to get back to work?"

I thought of the meeting I had set up with Dana to go over some marketing stuff. I didn't want to cancel, but I knew Dana wouldn't want me to miss a date. So I figured I would text her and tell her that there was a change of plans.

"Sounds good to me, lead the way."

We hoped in our golf cart which I insisted on driving, much to Ty's disappointment, and then looked down at my clothes. "Do I have time to change?"

"You look fine."

"You sure?"

"Again, you could wear a paper bag and—"

"You would still find me beautiful, I know, I know," I said it as if I were tired of hearing him say that. But honestly, it never grew old. Mostly because I knew it wasn't a line… he meant it.

It felt good to feel secure in a relationship. It felt good to feel as if I could trust his word. I didn't doubt Ty's feelings for me at all. I had asked for transparency and that was what I had received. Even though I had been burned before, something about him made me feel as if I could trust him. And I simply did.

Once we left the golf course, we went to the outdoor theatre in a clearing in a community filled with walking trails under a canopy of forest. Trees stretched for miles on each side and in the midst of them was the clearing situated on a slight hill where at least fifty people had already gathered to see this evening's show. It was just beginning to get dark when we arrived. And on our way there, Ty had insisted on stopping at his home to grab a blanket for us to sit on. I was glad he had because about time we reached the play all the lawn seats in front of the stage were taken and the only room that remained was on the hill overlooking the stage. We made our way up there, placed the blanket on the lawn, and sat down. Quickly, we realized that tonight's show wasn't a play at all but an opera.

"This is my first opera," I admitted in a hushed tone. I didn't want to disturb the other people around me even though the nearest person was like eight feet away.

"How are you liking it so far?"

"I'm enjoying it. It's not boring at all."

He laughed. "You expected it to be boring?"

"Well, yeah, once I realized it was an opera and not like a children's play or something."

"You thought I was taking you to see a children's play?"

"Well, I sort of thought it would be since you know... it's free and all."

He nodded in understanding. "These are professionals. Some sort of art endowment pays for the performance."

"Ah, that explains it. Wealthy donors."

"My grandparents donated. I heard even once upon a time, my mom wanted to be an opera singer."

"Whatever happened to her?" I asked softly.

At first, I didn't think he had heard me.

"She died of liver cirrhosis. She pretty much drank herself to death." He cleared his throat. "And Dad, before you ask, he's still around. He started another family."

"You have siblings out there?" I asked, not wanting to focus on his mother's death. No matter how he felt about her, I was sure it was hard for him to lose her.

His face spread into a smile, and I was relieved that I had asked him a question that hadn't caused him pain. "I do. Just one. A sister. She's about eighteen now."

"So you've met her?"

He nodded. "Definitely. I had already moved out of my grandparents' home before my dad remarried, but he would bring her over for certain holidays, so I would always visit when he did."

"You never went to his home?" I knew I was probably asking too much, but I was curious to know more about him. And the type of parents we had impacted us so much.

"Dad's?" He shook his head. "I'm afraid I'm not the

forgiving kind. If it hadn't been for my sister, I wouldn't have had anything to do with him. And he knew that."

"I'm sorry." I really was. Among all my friends, we all had rocky relationships with our parents.

"It is what it is. I just moved forward promising myself that I wouldn't make the same mistakes."

"And you haven't. You're Mr. Perfect. A doctor. An upstanding citizen. Running your own business. Successful by anyone's standards."

"Successful yes, but far from perfect," he said, directing his eyes back to the stage. Something about the way he made that last statement gave me pause. I shrugged it off. He was just being humble or just dealing with his own demons. Either way, I let the subject drop. I sensed that the mood of the evening had changed. It had gone from fun and light to a bit more intense than we both obviously wanted to deal with.

I let my attention focus on the opera in front of me. I was surprised by how much I enjoyed it. I had always thought I would find it boring, but the colors, the plot, the sheer brilliance of the lead singer's voice all told a story that I couldn't pull away from. My experience reminded me of that one scene in the movie "Pretty Woman" when Julia Roberts cried during the opera. I didn't think I was at that point of being moved to tears, but I was enjoying it, which made me smile.

"It's really good, isn't it?"

I glanced at him and nodded. "I have no idea what they're saying, but I love it."

He smiled and gestured to his lap. "You can lie in my lap, I don't bite."

And so I did, and I sighed in contentment as I watched the opera and Ty stroked my hair. I felt a drop of water touch my face and then another one. And before I knew it, rain drops were unleashed from the sky.

People sprinted away as torrential rain fell abruptly bringing our peaceful evening to an end. Ty grabbed my hand, I grabbed the blanket and together we took off running toward our car.

It wasn't until we got there that we realized somewhere along the way he had lost the key. We were getting soaked, so I grabbed his hand and raced toward a large cypress tree. We huddled under it and tossed the blanket on top of us.

The rain had slowed down, but I couldn't see much around or in front of us. The moon was barely a blimp in the sky, but under the tree at least we had some shelter.

"Thanks for showing me such a lovely evening."

He laughed. "Are you saying you aren't enjoying being soaking wet and stuck under a tree in the woods?"

"Hmmm... let me think about it. I'm going to have to go with no."

We huddled together, waiting for the rain to pass. His arm was wrapped around me. I rested my head against his shoulder, and he slowly ran his hand idly through my wet hair.

"This is kind of romantic," I found myself saying.

"Great... because this was all part of my plan."

"Oh? So you control the weather too?"

"Yes, in my free time."

I snuggled up closer to him and inhaled the scent of his neck before placing a kiss there. Something about the moment was kind of romantic. He looked down at me, took my chin in his hand and kissed me back. I sighed as his lips covered mine. And I groaned as his hands found their way under my shirt.

I wasn't wearing a bra, and the thin layer of my shirt hadn't been hiding much especially after we had gotten wet.

His fingers rubbed against my nipples, and I could barely breathe at the feel of his touch. He continued to fondle my breasts as the rain stopped and droplets of water trailed down my face. He kissed those droplets as his hands made magic beneath my top.

I reached for his pants, trying to get him out of his shorts as he pushed my skirt up and my thighs apart. He knelt between my thighs and started kissing me down below, pushing my panties to the side, licking the folds of my sex with his tongue and sucking on my clit with his warm mouth.

I groaned, not caring that we could get caught at any moment. The rain was clearing, but in the darkness of the night, I didn't think anyone could see what was going on just feet from the parking lot.

And a lot was going on. Ty ripped off my panties and tossed them somewhere among the bushes. He unzipped his pants, a feat I hadn't been able to accomplish in my prone position, then he climbed on top of me. He didn't waste any time pushing into me. I wrapped my arms around his shoulders and cried out as he drove into me over and over.

There under the tree, I tried to spread my legs even further, granting him better access so that he could go deeper. I wrapped my legs around his waist and tossed my head back in ecstasy as he filled me. The pleasure was intense as my inner muscles shivered around his thick shaft. He slid in and out of my wetness, keeping a steady pace as if he could keep this up forever. I moaned and greedily thrust my hips up to meet every stroke.

I let go of his shoulders and gripped the roots of the tree around me, my nails clinging to the dirt. This was hot. Public place. In the rain. On the ground. It was wild, uncivilized, and I loved every bit of it.

I groaned as he continued to push inside of me, pulling out just for a second, not completely, and then pushing back in. My senses were exploding from the rain against my skin, and Ty's hot kisses as he sheathed himself in my wetness. In the moonlight, I came, my hips driving up as Ty pushed into me one last time, hoarsely crying out as the pleasure of our lovemaking sent him spiraling over the edge.

He slowly pulled out of me and helped me up and off the ground. He peeked around the tree and said, "We can probably sneak away now without anyone noticing us."

I gestured toward his fly and he was like, "Oh," as he busily straightened his clothes. I giggled as I looked at him. He was covered in mud.

"It looks like you were mud wrestling and lost."

He laughed and helped me right my clothing, "Babe, you don't look much better."

Dusting myself off, I took a look at my clothes. I was covered in mud. Maybe he was right, but I wasn't going to admit it. I could feel mud caked to my butt, but refused to acknowledge it.

He tried to dust me off, but mud was caked in my hair, on my back, my legs, everywhere. He laughed and then I started to laugh and that's when a light shone on us, bringing our laughter to an abrupt end.

Instantly, Ty stepped in front of me. Blocking whomever was shining their light on me from seeing me.

"What are you two doing back here?" came an authoritative-sounding voice. If I had to guess, I would assume it was a cop or security. "The show was rained out, so all of you have to go."

"We were just looking for my keys, officer. We lost them in the rain."

"You lost your keys back here while it was raining? How exactly?" He clearly didn't believe us, but I didn't blame him. "Find your keys and then head home. I'll be in the parking lot if you need me." With that, the cop turned around and left.

"I guess we better find those keys," I said, moving toward the hill where we had fled which seemed eons ago but in truth, it had been fifteen minutes at most.

He turned on the flashlight of his cell phone and attempted to find the key. We were lucky that we remembered exactly where we'd sat because that's where we found the keys.

He grabbed them, and I said a thankful prayer in my head. But then upon closer inspection he realized that his car key was no longer on the key chain.

"Great," he said bitterly.

"This sucks..."

"I'll call a ride-share."

Less than ten minutes later, we were in the back of a ride-share driven by a kid who didn't look to be over sixteen-years-old.

"So what happened to you guys?" he said, not bothering to just ignore the fact that we were covered in mud.

"We're professional mud wrestlers," Ty said, and I pinched him.

"Cool," the kid said, dropping the subject.

In the darkness, Ty took my hand and leaned my head against his shoulder. It was unexpected, but covered in mud, in the darkness of a stranger's car, all I could think of was how happy I was.

9

woke up next to Ty, his arms wrapped around my middle. We spent many mornings waking up the same way. In fact, I spent more time at his home than I did my own nowadays. My houseplants were starting to hate me.

I could feel him pressed against me and I turned over, ready to engage in an early morning romp.

"Morning," he said, sleepily tracing his hands over my hip.

"Morning," I said, pushing him over and climbing on top of him. He was already hard.

"You're insatiable," he said as I slowly lowered myself onto his waiting shaft. Loving the way he stretched me, filled me. And still wet from our activities from earlier that evening, he slid into my wetness easily.

"I think I might be addicted to you," I breathed. Who was I kidding? I was more than addicted. I was in love.

AN HOUR LATER, we had showered and dressed. Ty was heading out to a conference, and I planned to work from home. He placed a kiss on my temple as he made me breakfast.

I was sure I had gained at least five pounds since I started spending so much time at Ty's house. What could I say? He was a good cook.

"You know you could stay here and get your work done instead of heading all the way home," he said as he mixed pancake batter and added fresh blueberries. My mouth watered. I was starving. I reached for an apple, hoping that would help fill me up so that I wouldn't scarf down ten pancakes in one sitting. I wasn't a huge fan of moderation. I couldn't get enough pancakes. And I couldn't get enough of Ty.

I thought about his offer, but also considered all the things I had to get done today. I planned to meet up with Dana and Becca for another event at Meredith's school. I couldn't do that if I was all the way on the other side of town.

"It's fine, I need to meet up with Dana and Becca anyway. We're going to an event at the school. Are you going to be there?"

He looked up and said, "Danny didn't mention anything nor did his mom."

And then it clicked. "Hold on. How are you Danny's uncle?" According to Ty, he didn't have a sibling besides his sister. And Danny's mom was too old to be Ty's sister, right?

"I'm not," he said. "I'm just a friend of his mom's family. Danny's mom and I grew up together. She lived next door. So after her divorce, when her deadbeat husband stopped showing up to events, I stepped in and started helping out with Danny."

"That was really kind of you," I said, meaning it.

He tossed some pancake batter on the griddle and said, "It's no big deal. She would have done the same for me. You know, my grandparents would have her babysit me even though we're practically the same age?" He chuckled as he flipped the pancakes.

"They thought she was the mature one, I guess."

"She was just a tattle-tale. A superior snitch."

He finished up the pancakes and then ate quickly. I gathered my things, and together we made our way to the lobby of his complex. We parted ways after exchanging a kiss. I was about to open my car door when I heard him call my name.

I turned around. "Can't get enough of me, huh?"

He smiled and said, "That's a reasonable assumption."

He reached into his pocket and said, "I've got something for you."

I looked at him questioningly when he pulled a keychain out of his pocket and pressed it into my hand. "This way you can come and go as you please."

"Oh, okay," I responded, not sure what else to say. Was he asking me to move in with him? Or was he just giving me his key? I was confused, but then I thought I was being silly. Of course, he wasn't asking me to move in with him... right?

"See you later," he said, kissing me again on my cheek and then hurrying off. I stood there for a while just staring at the key in my hand, and then finally I willed my legs to move.

I immediately called Dana. "I need your help."

"I thought we were meeting up today. We're still on, right? You aren't blowing me off again to lie in bed with Mr. Lover Boy, are you?"

"I promise you, I'm up and out of bed. But Mr. Lover Boy, as you called him, gave me a key to his condo? What does it mean? Does he want me to move in with him?"

"Did he say that he wanted you to move in with him?"

"Well, no…"

"Then why would you think he wants you to move in with him?"

I felt sort of stupid suddenly for jumping to conclusions. "You're right. I don't know what I was thinking."

"He probably just gave you the key because you're always shacking up there."

"Hey."

"Well, you are always there; I'm just saying."

"Well, enough said. I'll see you in a few hours. Don't be late."

I hung up and tried not to feel foolish. Dana was right; unless he explicitly asked me to move in with him, why would I assume that, that's what he wanted?

I wanted to kick myself. Sometimes I leapt to conclusions without even the slightest provocation. I was the queen of making assumptions.

I was on autopilot as I made my way to my house. My mind went from thinking of Ty to thinking about the key he had given me. I guess I sort of did want to move in with him. Yeah, our relationship was new. But I felt that I knew him well, and I did want to spend all my time with him. And clearly, he felt the same way, right? If he had given me a key and told me to come and go as I pleased. That meant something. Or was I just being silly? I couldn't tell.

I worked at home until I heard Dana ring my doorbell. *She was early,* I thought to myself.

"I need to use your bathroom, now," were the first words out of her mouth as soon as I opened the door.

She was carrying just a plastic bag. Where was her laptop?

She didn't even give me a chance to respond. She just marched past me, and then I heard a door shutting hard.

"Umm... okay then," I said mostly to myself since Dana wasn't around to hear. I wondered what was up with her.

About five minutes later, she came out the bathroom and sank down on my couch and said, "Now we wait."

I didn't know what she was talking about.

"Hey," she said suddenly, "is this the same couch Carter and I defiled?"

"God no, I got rid of it."

She shrugged. "That was probably for the best."

I sat down across from her in the recliner I had bought from a thrift store. It was super comfortable. I tossed my feet up and looked at my best friend. "Can you tell me why you charged into my house, and what exactly are we waiting for?"

"I think I'm late."

I looked at my cell phone. "No, you're not. Actually, you're—"

She sent me a pointed look. And I instantly felt so stupid. "Ohh, you mean late *late*. As in laaaaatttteeee."

She nodded.

"Oh my god, what are you going to do with four kids?"

"Shut up, Piper."

"You can barely keep up with the three you have now. You tell me that on a constant basis. And what if you're having twins or even triplets this time around?"

A throw pillow collided with my face, and Dana growled, "Shut up, Piper."

"How can I shut up? This is great news"

"Really? I haven't slept in like a decade."

"Sleep is overrated."

"You sleep in every day."

"Yeah, I love being childless."

She shot me a glare, and I held back a giggle. And then she abruptly turned away from me, and my grin fell. Her shoulders began to shake. Dana was crying.

Instantly, I got up and sat down on the couch next to her. I embraced her, and she just rested her head against my shoulder and cried.

I didn't say a word. I just let her cry it all out. I didn't bother with platitudes or try to tell her everything would be alright. I knew my friend better than that, and she wouldn't appreciate or tolerate being placated.

When she was done, she wiped the tears from her cheeks and wiped her nose on her sleeve. I pretended not to notice.

"I'm sorry," she said.

"You don't have to apologize."

She sniffled again. "I'm just feeling a little overwhelmed. I know if I am pregnant that I'll love this one as much as Meredith and the twins, but oh God, the thought of breastfeeding again. Or weaning or potty training just makes me so tired."

"Just hire a nanny this time."

She instantly perked up. "That's a great idea. Why didn't I think of that when the twins were born?"

I shrugged. "Glad I could be of help; now do you want me to come with you?"

She shook her head and stood up. She pushed her shoulders back and puffed out her chest as if she were going into battle. "I can do this. I am a strong, fearless woman completely capable of handling any task given to me. Including having and raising another baby."

"Or babies..."

"Shut up, Piper." With that, she walked away.

A minute later I heard an excited whoop and then she strolled in with a big smile on her face. "Negative."

"Congratulations."

"Thank God, I was about to lose my mind for a second. If I have to look at one more diaper, I think I would scream..." She chewed on her lip and looked regretful for a second. "But it would have been nice to have a fourth."

I shook my head. "You don't know what you want."

"Yeah, I do. A beer. That was close call. Got any?" I gestured to the fridge and then heard her say a minute later, "Piper, you're a disappointment. The strongest thing you have in your fridge is this apple juice that smells rancid."

"Sorry," I said, not really sorry. "I haven't gone shopping in at least a week."

"Don't you eat any more?" Dana asked, coming back into the living room empty handed.

"Ty cooks all the time or we go out—"

"Oh yeah, tell me about this whole key situation."

"There's not much to tell," I said, feeling sort of ridiculous that I had made a big deal of it. "It's just a matter of convenience."

"Hmm... you two sure are getting close."

I shrugged. "I guess."

"So do you think he's the one?"

"I don't really believe in that."

"Oh, please, of course you do. You're a diehard romantic."

"I am not."

"Yes you are."

"Am not."

"Oh gosh, now we sound like the kids."

I got up. Not wanting to tell Dana how I really felt. My track record wasn't great, and I wanted to be totally sure about Ty before I went around singing his praises to everyone who would listen. Not that I didn't do that already...

"You know it's okay to fall in love, Piper." She looked concerned.

I laughed it off. "In love? I'm not in love, I just really like him."

"That's okay too. I don't want you to feel as if you're going to be judged for falling in love again."

"Well, it does feel that way... I mean, not by you, but I'm my biggest critic, Dana. I can't be trusted to make any decisions of the heart because I always mess up. No matter how hard I try to get things right, I fail over and over. I compulsively fail. Maybe in some ways, I'm a failure."

"No you're not. You run a very successful business, you built this house almost from the studs up, and you're a great aunt. Nothing about who you are says failure."

"Well, everything about my track record in love says I'm a failure."

"You're being too hard on yourself. Everyone makes mistakes of the heart. It's called being human."

"It's called being stupid."

"You really need to stop beating yourself up over your past romances. They're in the past. Let them stay there."

I sighed. "Everything you're saying is absolutely right and logical, but I still feel defeated and unsure about myself when it comes to this kind of stuff. Like what if my family is just cursed to spend eternity in bad relationship after bad relationship."

"Yikes, then I hate to see who Meredith starts dating."

I knew she was being facetious, and that exasperated me. "I'm not joking, Dana. Sometimes I feel as if I'm just destined to keep making the same mistake. I don't want to trust the wrong man again and in the long run end up getting hurt or worse yet—end up hurting someone else I don't even know."

"That was a fluke, Piper. It's not as if every man you've dated was harboring some dark secret."

"That I know of..."

"Stop. You can't let a few bad apples spoil everything for you. Be positive and optimistic. Isn't that what you're always telling me?"

"Maybe that's bad advice."

"Who are you and what have you done with Piper?" she said, and I couldn't help but laugh.

"I would like to think that I've finally grown up."

"Well, don't do that. Unless you want to turn into me. I mean, have you seen my crows' feet yet?" she asked, pointing at the barely noticeable wrinkles at the edge of her eyes.

"You're beautiful and perfect. You don't have crows' feet."

"You're so sweet, that's why you're my best friend. You're way better of a person than I'll ever be."

"You're a good person too,"

She laughed harshly. "Only on the weekends when I get to sleep in." She stood up and said, "I need to run and get my laptop out of the car so that we can get started on work and then meet Becca back at the school… be back in a sec."

While she was gone, I thought of what she said. I had frequently downplayed how I felt about Ty when talking to my friends. I really did feel as if at any moment the proverbial other shoe would drop and then I would be back at square one: loveless, alone, and feeling sorry for myself.

And it wasn't that I didn't trust Ty. I just didn't really trust myself.

Soon enough Dana came back in, and I focused the next few hours to listening to her marketing plans for my business. Dana was clearly good at her job, and I felt lucky to have her help. I told her as much. She had just shrugged and said, "It's the least I could do after all you've done for me and Meredith over the years."

We wrapped up what we were doing and headed to the school. On the way there she asked me if I had any dinner plans for the night. I figured that I would give Ty a day off of cooking and told Dana that I would be glad to accompany her and her family to dinner.

"We're having spaghetti. Be warned. Only one kid knows how to use utensils properly, so if some spaghetti goes flying across the table and lands in your lap, don't take it personally."

"Duly noted. I won't."

After the school event, I looked at my phone and realized that I hadn't reached out to Ty all day. I had a text from him though. "What would you like for dinner tonight?"

"Having dinner with Dana."

"Oh," he said, followed by a frowning emoji.

I laughed. "I'm giving you a break," I texted back.

"I like cooking for you," he replied.

"You're sweet."

I smiled and put my phone down and then another text popped up. "You have my key. Swing by when you're done with dinner. I miss you already."

Feeling warm and fuzzy inside, I texted back, "I miss you too."

THE DAY WENT by faster than I expected and the next thing I knew, I was helping Carter and Meredith put away the dishes whilst Dana got the twins ready for bed. Dinner had been yummy. Nothing fancy like Ty made but homey and filling.

"So how's your love life?" Carter asked when

Meredith was out of earshot. "Dana said you're dating some guy and you're in love?"

I blushed. "I'm not in love, I'm just trying to see where this all goes."

"Yeah, there's nothing wrong with being cautious."

"Thank you. Now explain that to your wife."

He shook his head. "No thanks. I don't want her to bite my head off. You know how she gets when she swears she's right."

"Are we talking about Mom?" Meredith asked, popping back into the kitchen. "If so, you're so right, Carter; Mom hates to be wrong. She's like allergic to it or something."

We all started laughing and abruptly stopped when we heard someone clearing their throat. "I'm glad you guys are having a good laugh at my expense."

Carter quickly walked over and embraced Dana, putting his chin on the top of her head as he gave us all as secret smile. "No one's laughing at you, sweetheart, I assure you. "

"Yeah, Mom," Meredith said with a straight face, "we're just laughing with you."

"Funny, I didn't hear myself laughing."

"Imagine that," I said, smothering a giggle.

"So what are we talking about?" she asked from her husband's embrace. I envied them. They loved each other always and just always knew it. Well, Carter always knew it. It was Dana who had taken awhile to come around.

"We're talking about Auntie Piper's love life. Apparently, Infinity Connections is working out."

I nodded. "Did you know that Danny's uncle isn't really his uncle?"

"Huh?" she said, clearly not knowing what I was talking about.

"Danny's uncle, Ty, the guy I'm dating."

"Ohhhh you hit it off with Ty. That's even better. He thinks you're hot, and he's the president of Infinity Connections."

My good mood came crashing down. There was no way. I must have misheard her. "Hold on, Meredith. What did you just say?"

She looked at me curiously. "Which part? The part about Ty being the president of Infinity?"

"Yeah," I said hoarsely. "Who told you that?"

"Danny did. That's why his mother was able to go on so many free dates. She didn't pay anything because Ty owns the company."

I heard all I needed to hear. "Carter, Dana, thanks for having me." I hugged Meredith. "I think I'm going to head home."

Fighting back tears and ignoring their confused glances, I grabbed my purse in the living room and made my way to my car.

As I crossed the street, I heard Dana call out to me, "Piper, wait. What's wrong? I saw your face back there. What's going on?"

"I didn't know Ty was the president of Infinity."

"What do you mean?"

I took a deep breath and tried not to cry. "He never mentioned that to me. Not once."

"I don't understand. What's the big deal? Why are you upset?"

I explained to her how he had told me that I was his match and how he had only recently signed up for the agency. "He lied to me, Dana. And played with my love life. He preyed on me. On my desire to be loved."

Dana shook her head. "I'm sure there's another explanation."

I shrugged, feeling crushed. "There could be another explanation, but not one I'm willing to hear."

She caught my arm as I turned to get in my car. "At least talk to him first, Piper. Like I said, there's probably a reasonable explanation."

"What excuse could he possibly give me that will make me feel better about his lies?" I said, more to myself than to Dana.

"You're right," was all she said. She let go of me, and I slid into the driver's seat.

"I'll call you."

I drove away and kept the tears at bay for about a

block. And then I couldn't see from the blur of tears, so I pulled over in front of a house and just sobbed into my hands.

How could he? How could he do this to me? How could he lie to me? He knew about my past. Apparently, he knew everything there was to know about me. If he was the president then he had access to my file, and clearly he had read it. He knew everything about me and I knew next to nothing about him.

I didn't stop to think. I didn't bother to call. I just drove straight to his home. I wanted answers, and I wanted them now.

I rode up the elevator to his condo. I let myself in. Happy that he wasn't there yet. I didn't know where he was, but I figured he would be home soon.

I couldn't help myself then. I sat down and started going through his stuff. I knew it was wrong. But I was hurting, and he wasn't there yet to give me answers. And I doubted when he did arrive that his answers would be truthful.

I didn't think I could trust him. No. I knew I couldn't trust him. Unfortunately, he didn't really have any personal information just laying around in his home. I opened his laptop and searched the Internet for his company. Besides the website, there wasn't much about the company online, and the "About Us" section didn't include the company's founder's name or anything else relating to its workers. But then I googled him and there were pictures of him and Sylvia at a charity function for Alzheimer's. *So much for having just met,* I thought wryly to myself. Wasn't that what he had told me? That he didn't know Sylvia well. I couldn't remember, since I couldn't separate the truth from his lies.

And as I continued looking, I found a whole profile of him on a career networking page and several other websites. In each case, he was listed as the CEO of Infinity Connections. So he hadn't bothered to really hide anything, I guess because he never thought I would look.

And he was right. I had been naïve again. I had trusted a man while knowing next to nothing about his past. I had made the same mistake again. No, I was wrong. This wasn't the same mistake. I hadn't loved my ex who cheated on me. I could barely remember his name. But I had fallen in love with Ty. Or, at least, I had fallen in love with the man who I had thought he was. And boy, I couldn't have been more wrong.

What had he thought? What had his plan been? String me along and dump me? It was almost creepy that he'd orchestrated this whole ruse. And for what? What had he wanted from me? Besides to deceive me and humiliate me?

In frustration, I wiped at the tears that were falling

down my cheeks. I didn't have the luxury of being sad; I needed to stay focused, I needed to stay mad.

I heard the door opening and tried to regain my composure. He came in and smiled upon seeing me. "I see you used your key."

I nodded, unable to speak.

He didn't notice as he undid his tie. He was still wearing his work clothes.

"How was the conference?" I forced myself to ask.

"Your voice sounds funny. Are you okay?"

"I don't know. Am I? After all, you know everything about me. You should be able to figure it out."

He looked at me strangely and said again, "Are you okay?"

"Wonderful. Now that the blinders are off and I know what type of man you really are."

He shook his head. "I'm not following. What's wrong?" He reached for my arm, and I snatched it away and stood up.

"Why didn't you just tell me the truth? Why did you lie to me? Was all this just a game to you?"

"I don't know what you're talking about."

"Are you saying that you've been perfectly honest with me? This whole time?"

He stared at me, as if trying to figure out what I was talking about. "I honestly don't know why you're angry with me. I'm no good at guessing games," he said, sounding frustrated. "I just know that you're angry with me, but I honestly have no idea why. Please tell me what's going on."

"Two words," I growled, "Infinity Connections."

"What about it?" he said, not missing a beat.

"When did you plan to tell me that you owned it?"

He sighed. "So that's what this is all about?"

I shook my head, not sure why he was so nonchalant about my anger. "You lied to me, Ty."

He shook his head. "I didn't."

"You said you were my match, my date that night... but you weren't. Were you?"

He shook his head. "You've got it all wrong, Piper. I was your date that night."

"Oh really? I just happened to be matched with the president of the dating agency? Are you going to tell me that you're a client in your own company and we just happened to be matched with each other? Do you think I'm stupid or something?"

He pulled at his tie and angrily ripped it off. He swore in frustration. "I didn't want you to find out like this. Yes, I wasn't one hundred percent truthful—"

"Truth isn't based on percentages, Ty. Either you tell the truth or you don't. There aren't any shades of gray when it comes to being a liar."

He sat down and shook his head. He looked up at me and gave me a pleading look. "Listen, I admit, I did lead you to believe that I was a client instead of the owner, but I knew we were building something together and that would have been ruined if I had told you the truth right away."

"So you lied to me instead? To be clear, Ty, whatever you thought we were building was being built on lies. And I'm done listening to yours."

I grabbed my purse and was about to walk out the door when he grabbed my arm. "Why does it matter how we ended up together? As long as we're with each other that's all that you should care about."

"Just listen to yourself, do you really believe that?"

He nodded. "Yes, I do." His gaze burned into my own. "So what, I bent the truth a little? I was going to tell you eventually."

"I don't believe you."

"Piper—"

"You honestly don't understand that what you did was wrong, do you? You manipulated me, Ty."

"No I didn't—"

"You did. By starting a relationship with me based on lies; by leading me to think something was true when it wasn't... You lied to me... manipulated me into having a relationship with you, and the best you can say is that you were going to tell me eventually?" I held back tears. "God, you must have had a great laugh reading my evaluation and my relationship history."

"I would never laugh at you, Piper. I respect you too much to—"

"Stop," I said, putting a hand against his chest. "Stop with the lies. You don't respect me. Because if you respected me you would have told me the truth. If you had respected me you wouldn't have led me on, you wouldn't have straight out lied to me about being my match, about only knowing Sylvia a short time."

He shook his head and opened his mouth to deny it all, but I wasn't going to listen. "You manipulated me, Ty. You lied to me to get what you wanted. That's not what you do to someone you care about."

I stormed out of his condo. I was so upset that my stomach felt like it was tied in knots. I took the elevator down to the ground floor, my heart beating triple time, scared that Ty was going to meet me at the ground floor, and convince me to listen to him, but also afraid that he wouldn't. That he didn't care enough to stop me from walking out of his life. I held my breath as the elevator door opened.

No one. No one was there. I quickly walked out of the building and got into my car. I held the tears at bay until I was home and then as soon as my door was shut and locked, I let myself sob.

I was done with love.

10

Dana shook her head as she digested all that I had just told her. She had pretty much forced a confession out of me. I had spent the past week in bed, barely doing any work, hiding from the world, and she had knocked on my door for like an hour straight until I opened it.

She had alternated between yelling, "I know you're in there," and "Don't make me kick this door down."

When she had actually started kicking the door, I had opened it. And to my surprise, I had also found Becca outside. She had jumped out of the car as soon as I opened the door and had apologized for Dana's behavior.

"I told her not to kick the door," she'd said, giving me an apologetic look.

Now Becca was in my kitchen, making herself a sandwich, while I told them my sad tale.

"At least you didn't marry him," Becca said, sitting down before taking a big bite.

"Yeah, she has a point." Dana nodded sagely.

I put my head down on the dining room table and groaned. "I'm so stupid... so, so stupid."

"Don't beat yourself up," Becca said.

"It's not worth it," Dana added, "Trust us. We were pretty much betrayed by the same man."

"Actually, you were betrayed," Becca pointed out much to Dana's annoyance. "I was just sort of used." She frowned and then took another bite before saying with her mouth full, "You know I'm not too sure which one is worse."

I raised my head and looked at the two of them. "You guys are off topic. We're supposed to be talking about me. Remember?"

Becca hurriedly apologized. "I'm sorry, Piper. It's like you can't trust anyone. That's why I don't date. Men just aren't worth it."

Dana shook her head and said to Becca, "You're too young to be so cynical."

Becca sighed. "It's no use. I read a blog about it. All the good ones are taken. And even if they weren't, apparently even the good ones go rotten. I mean, look what happened to Piper. We all thought Ty was the good guy, but nope—he sucks just like all the others."

I raised my head and said, "You guys aren't making this any better."

They looked at each other and instantly looked guilty. "We're sorry," Becca offered.

"I'm not really," Dana said.

I sighed heavily and stood up and rummaged through my refrigerator. "Where's the stupid ice cream when you need it?" I mumbled to myself.

Becca perked up. "There's ice cream?"

"Nope," I said, feeling dejected.

"I'll go get some," Dana offered. "What's the use of a pity party without ice cream? Be right back, ladies." She grabbed her car keys and went out the door. I went and sat back down across from Becca and just stared at the wall.

"I'm really sorry that things between you and Ty didn't work out," she said once she finally finished her sandwich.

"I just wish he had been honest with me from the start. Why would he lie and manipulate me?"

Becca didn't answer. She just listened.

"Sometimes I wonder if there's something wrong with me."

"There's nothing wrong with you—"

"Then why do I keep making the same mistake?

Trusting the wrong men?" Becca didn't offer an answer, just a sympathetic ear, so I continued, "I can't keep blaming others for my mistakes. In the past what? Six months? I've dated three different men who have lied to me, and the only one who was decent to me I dumped." I let out a laugh of contempt at myself.

"Stop beating yourself up... you didn't know... stop blaming yourself. We all make mistakes."

I shook my head. "I don't just make mistakes... I make the same mistakes over and over. I'm as bad as my brother."

Becca shook her head. "I was married to him, remember? There's no comparison. He's not a good person, Piper. But you are. He hurts people while you just want to be loved. Don't compare yourself to him. You're nothing like him."

I got up and went to the window and looked out. "My parents were rotten at love. Maybe that's why my brother and I are so dysfunctional."

"Your brother is dysfunctional because that's who he's chosen to be. No one's predestined to be a jerk."

She had a point, but I wasn't ready to let myself off the hook yet. I knew Becca was kind of right, but I still blamed myself. Sylvia had said I deserved love, but now I wasn't so sure.

* * *

Hours after Becca and Dana had gone home, I heard a knock at my door.

"I don't want any more ice cream!" I yelled, assuming it was them again. I had to practically kick them out earlier since they hadn't wanted to leave me sad and alone.

The knock sounded again, and I reluctantly got up to answer it. *Probably just solicitors,* I thought to myself. Someone probably wanted to sell me a new security system or cookies or something.

I looked out the peephole and saw Ty standing there. My heartbeat picked up. What was he doing here?

I could ignore him or I could yell at him through the door. It was a hard decision, but I went with the path of least resistance.

I crouched down low and crawled away from my door, so he wouldn't see my shadow from outside the window.

Like an idiot, I crawled from my door to my living room, trying not to make any noise. I wasn't sure what I was thinking; after all, he knew I was there, my car was parked out front. And hadn't I just yelled at him before I realized who was there.

I sat down in front of my couch and just hoped he would give up and go away.

"I'm not going away!" he yelled loud enough for me to hear.

Oh. Well, so much for wishful thinking.

"You can open the door or I can make a scene. It's your choice."

"You wouldn't!" I yelled from my position on the floor. I scrambled to get up as he continued to knock obnoxiously on my door while calling my name over and over.

I didn't want anyone to call the cops. My HOA would be so mad. They took pride in the cops not showing up in our neighborhood. First I had Dana hollering at my door and now Ty. I was sure my neighbors were not happy with me.

I abruptly opened the door and yelled at him, "Go away, I have nothing to say to you. And if you keep banging on my door, I'll call the cops."

"Call them. I don't care."

I could tell from the fiery expression on his face that he meant it. "Then I guess you're going to be escorted away in a police car."

I picked up my phone, ready to call the non-emergency number, but I didn't know it and there was no way I was going to call 911. I might be a little flighty and prone to bad judgment, but even I wouldn't waste police resources on getting my ex to get off my doorstep.

Apparently, he didn't know that. "I understand if you want to call the cops on me. Just give me a minute to say my part, and then I'll leave you alone. I just want you to hear me out."

I lowered my phone, but kept it in my hand.

"Can I come in?" he asked.

"No. You can say whatever it is you have to say from there."

"Okay..." he looked at me and then shifted uncomfortably from foot to foot. I had never seen Ty uncomfortable before. I hadn't had the privilege of seeing him nervous and unsure of himself. I had to admit, it made me feel slightly better. But just slightly.

"So what do you have to say? You're sorry? You didn't mean to lie to me? It's all just one big misunderstanding?"

He shook his head. "Nothing I felt for you was a lie—"

I sent him a chilled look before interrupting, "Try again."

"I'm serious. Maybe my methods were questionable, but—"

I couldn't believe the words coming out of his mouth. "Your methods were questionable? This isn't some sort of scientific study, Ty. This was real life, not some sort of experiment!"

"I know that—"

"No. I don't think you do. I bet you're so used to

controlling every aspect of your life that you thought you could control me too."

"Piper, it's not like that at all."

"Oh really? So you're telling me you didn't deliberately manipulate me and mislead me?"

He faltered. "I'm not going to pretend that what I did was right—"

"Good."

"But my intentions were not to hurt you."

"And what exactly were your intentions, Ty? Because the only thing you succeeded in doing was hurting and humiliating me."

"Again," he said, growing agitated, "that was not my intention."

"It doesn't matter what your intentions were... all that matters is that you've shown me your true colors. You're a liar. You manipulated me to get what you wanted. And I'm not going to let you manipulate me anymore. We're done talking—"

"No. No we aren't. I'm not going to give up on us."

"There is no us."

He raised his eyebrows.

"I have nothing to say to you. All you've done is lie to me."

"That isn't true. The way I feel about you, none of that was a lie."

I ignored the lump that formed in my throat. I didn't

want to talk about emotions. I needed to hate him now because hating him would keep me from forgiving him. And I needed to keep my distance and protect myself. I couldn't allow myself to forgive him and risk him hurting me all over again. "You pretended to be someone you weren't."

"I never pretended."

"Fine, then you omitted the truth. Whatever you call it. It's still dishonest. You played with me. Played games with my love life."

I could tell he was growing frustrated. "What I feel for you is not a game. It's very real, and you know that. So please, stop with the victim mentality." Suddenly he looked angry.

"Excuse me?" I placed my hands on my hips as if warning him to consider his next words carefully. How dare he?

"You heard me. You're making me out to be the villain just because that's the kind of guy you're used to dating. For the record, Piper, you chose those guys. You chose the worst of the worst."

"I did not choose to be cheated on."

"You sound like a broken record. What's the saying? When you do something over and over, it's not a mistake; it's a hobby."

I felt as if he had slapped me in the face. "How dare you judge me? You don't get close to anyone. You just sit behind your desk and play with the love lives of others. Promising happily ever after. But tell me something, Ty, do you even know what it is to be happy? I mean, after all, it's not like you had someone to teach you." I knew I had hit below the belt, but I was furious. Furious with myself for falling for him and furious with him for having orchestrated it all.

His mouth tightened, and he shook his head and muttered something to himself. Gone was the frustration and anger in his eyes, and in its place was hurt. He quickly looked away from me and took a visible breath. "I think we both just need to breathe and calm down. I'm sorry for what I just said. And I know you're angry. But just hear me out, can you do that?"

"No," I said holding back tears. "I've heard enough."

He didn't try to stop me from closing the door. His face showed resignation and hurt. But I didn't care, I was done caring. I shut the door and decided at that moment that I was also closing this chapter of my life... the chapter on love.

11

"Did you lose weight? Your clothes are barely fitting," Dana commented.

I looked down at my baggy shorts and t-shirt. I hadn't lost weight. If anything, I had put on a few pounds since I was stuffing my face every other hour it seemed. I thought I was depressed. Or maybe I was just really sad.

I was determined not to sit around thinking about Ty. In fact, whenever he came into my mind, I pushed him away. Since our encounter at my front door, he hadn't reached out to me. I felt disappointed that he hadn't tried harder. But maybe too much had been said between us.

In the end, I shrugged off Dana's question with a mumbled, "Maybe."

We were sitting around her kitchen table just me,

her, and Meredith. We were making a get well card for Meredith's teacher. Carter had taken the twins to the zoo, so we were on our own. I was having fun. At least I thought I was. I tried to not think too much about my emotions lately.

"Are you lovesick?" Meredith asked me while Dana went to find more scissors. *Who would have thought that making a card would turn into such a full-blown project?* I thought to myself as I glued little hearts all over the back of the card.

"Lovesick?" What had given Meredith that idea?

"Yeah, I read about it in a blog."

I rolled my eyes. "Is everyone reading blogs about relationships nowadays?"

"Um... yeah... aren't you?"

I shook my head. "Maybe that's why I'm such a disaster at love. I don't read enough about it."

She laughed. "Maybe. But you don't have to read about love to know what it is. You just know, you know?"

"I wish it were that simple."

"It is that simple," Meredith said. "You adults just make it so complicated. That's why I'm determined to never grow up."

"Good luck with that."

She smiled widely at me and then Dana appeared with a glue gun, glitter, and balls of yarn. *Were we making a card for every teacher in the school,* I was tempted to ask.

I stood up. "I feel like you guys can handle it from here. See you later, kid." I kissed Meredith's forehead as I gathered my things.

"Be right back, hon," Dana said, heading out with me. She never left a kid alone. She must have had something to say and didn't want Meredith to overhear.

"You're unhappy," she said without preamble.

I shrugged. "We can't be happy all the time."

"That's not the Piper I know."

"The Piper you know was immature and irresponsible. She made too many mistakes. I'm determined to not be that person anymore."

"Funny, the Piper I know is an entrepreneur, incredibly kind, and smart. She also has always been there for me. Never in a million years would I describe her as immature or irresponsible."

"You're my best friend, you're required to sing my praises. It's in the job description," I joked, but her words were moving, and I was trying to keep things light so that I wouldn't tear up. Dana and Carter had always been my biggest cheerleaders, and I appreciated them so much.

"I'm tired of watching you mope around."

"I'm not moping."

"You are. I thought after your initial meltdown that

you would be fine and return back to normal, but I was wrong. You can't bounce back because you're in love."

I scoffed. "I'm not in love with Ty. Far from it. I hate the guy."

"You don't hate him. He hurt you, but you don't hate him. In fact, I think you're so angry with yourself because even after he hurt you, you're still in love with him."

"You're way off base," I said, opening my car door, trying my best to quickly get away from her and this conversation that I didn't want to have. "I'll call you later."

I climbed in and started the car. She leaned into the window. "You know Meredith was right?"

"That we should have used the glue gun from the beginning? You're right."

"You know I'm not talking about arts and crafts. She's right about love being simple. I loved Carter since I met him, but I complicated things and for that reason, I wasted so many years of my life without him. Don't overthink love, Piper. Just go for it."

"But he betrayed me..."

"There's always two sides to every story. Talk to him and find out his."

I made a noncommittal sound and drove away. On my drive home, all I could think of was what Dana had said. And then it had me thinking back to the fight I had with Ty and what he had said. We had been really nasty toward each other. We had both said things that were pretty unforgivable. How could we possibly move past that?

And did I even want to? Did he want to? I didn't know. But I knew as I texted him that I was done being the victim as he so aptly called me. I wanted to take control over my love life. And this would be the first step. I had let so many different obstacles stop me from falling in love, like really in love.

I chose the worst not just because they wouldn't reject me, but also because with them I could hold back part of me. I hadn't held back with Ty. And truth be told no matter what happened I wouldn't be that scared person I had once been. I wouldn't be afraid to love. I wouldn't overcomplicate things. I would just let myself be loved. That was scary. Besides my friends, I felt that everyone else who loved me in my life had done so under certain conditions. I wanted to see more than anything if Ty could forgive me and love me unconditionally. I wouldn't accept anything else.

To my surprise, Ty texted me back immediately. "I can meet you tonight," he said. "Eight?"

"That's fine," I texted back.

That evening, I waited with bated breath for Ty to show up. I had changed clothes at least five times. I didn't want to look eager, but I also didn't want to look sloppy. I had specialized in sloppy over the past few weeks, and it was not a good look.

I put on a plain white cotton dress, a pair of sandals, and earrings in the shape of stars. I brushed my hair back into a ponytail and just waited for him.

At 8 o'clock sharp a knock sounded at my door. I had arranged for him to come over to my place so that we could talk in private, but now I was nervous at the thought of being around him. When I opened the door, that nervousness spiked. I was tongue-tied, so I just gestured for him to come in.

He was dressed as if he had just attended a meeting. He was wearing a suit and carrying a cross-body bag that seemed to be some sort of briefcase.

"You're a little overdressed, aren't you?"

He looked down at his clothes as he came in and smiled ruefully. "I came straight from the airport."

"Where were you when I texted you?"

"A conference in Atlanta."

"Oh," I said, surprised. "So you haven't had a chance to go home yet and change…"

"I figured this was more important," he said, looking at me as if trying to remember every detail, every feature. I was uneasy under his gaze. I felt raw and emotional now that he was standing here in front of me. But I also felt a weird emotion, one I could only describe as relief. He was here and for some reason, that made my world feel brighter. I knew that feeling was love.

I turned away from his penetrating stare and gestured for him to sit down.

He took off his bag and sat down at the kitchen table. "So you wanted to talk to me?"

"Yeah." I was unsure how to start. I opened my mouth to speak, but he was faster.

"I didn't expect you to contact me. Your text caught me by surprise."

"After what happened between us the last time we were together, I didn't think I would ever want to see you again."

He placed his hands on the table and folded them together. "After what I said and did, I wouldn't blame you."

"That's just it, I think we need to stop blaming each other."

"Is that your way of saying that I get a second chance?"

I shook my head. "This is just my way of saying that I'm ready to listen."

"I guess I'll take that for now."

"You'll have to because that's all I'm offering." Wow, I sounded tough. Where had this confident version of myself been hiding?

"I guess I'll start at the beginning."

"Please do."

"First of all, I never read your evaluation; Sylvia handles all that. I never violated your privacy..." He looked up at me, waiting for me to say something, but I wanted to hear more first. He continued, "When I met you at the school I had no idea you were a client."

"When did you find out?"

"Danny told me sometime before we went on our first date."

"Did you set up that disastrous date I went on with that Geoff guy?"

"Guilty as charged. When I found out that you were part of the agency, I did go into your account and change your match. I sort of hoped you would just give up on the agency then so that way it wouldn't be unethical for me to date you instead. Sylvia was pissed."

"She knew?"

He quickly backtracked. "She wasn't an accessory or anything. After she realized what I'd done, she was the one who threatened to tell you everything. That's why I showed up that night at the museum, to tell you the truth."

"Instead you said you were with the agency and that you were my date—"

"Which was all true..."

"A partial truth."

He nodded. "You're right. I wasn't completely

truthful because I didn't think you would react well and I was right."

"Yeah, sue me because I'm not a fan of being lied to. So when did you plan to tell me the truth?"

He shrugged. "Truthfully, I didn't have a plan. I was supposed to tell you that night at the museum exactly who I was. That was the only plan I had and when that fell through—"

"You mean when you deliberately failed to tell me who you were?"

"You're right about everything. I should have been forthcoming. I should have told you the truth. I don't know why I didn't. It's just everything was going so well, and I didn't want you to misconstrue my intentions."

"And what were your intentions?"

"To have you fall in love with me."

"Love can't be orchestrated."

He sighed and sat back. "Trust me. I know that now. If I could do it all again—"

"But you can't, so there's no reason to even go there."

He nodded again. "You're right. So where do we go from here?"

I shrugged. "I guess I could kick you out and say goodbye..."

His face hardened, and he moved to stand up. I reached out then and placed a hand over his. "Hold on, you didn't let me finish..."

"What were you going to say?"

"I was going to say I could kick you out of my house and out of my life, or I could forgive you and see where this goes..."

He entwined his fingers with my own and studied our hands linked together. "I was stupid. And arrogant. You were right, I had no right to play God with your love life. I should have told you I owned Infinity Connections. I should have been honest with you from the start. But I wasn't, and I know that's no way to start a relationship. I'm willing to put all my cards on the table. Be an open book."

He reached for his briefcase, never letting go of my hand, and pulled out his laptop. He opened it, accessed a file and said, "Read it."

I looked at him curiously. "What is it?"

"Everything about me. I had Sylvia send it all over once you texted me. It's all here. My family history. My evaluation, which Sylvia insisted I do, since she wanted me to understand exactly what we were requiring our clients to do. My likes, dislikes, greatest fears, favorite color. My W2s for the past four years, blood type, health records. I think Sylvia might have even included my college entrance exam scores. Passwords. Bank account information. You name it, it's there."

I smiled, I couldn't help it. I was amused.

"I just want you to know that I'm not hiding

anything from you. Nothing. Anymore. I'm an open book from now on. I'm done hiding, and that includes hiding how I feel. Just give me a chance. I might not deserve it, but I know if you give me the opportunity I would like to share everything with you, Piper." He took my other hand in his and said, "Look at me."

I stared into his eyes and saw love there. I teared up and wanted to look away, but I couldn't. His gaze held my own as if he never planned to let me go. With a steady voice he said, "Everything that I am and everything that I have is yours. You're my world."

I looked from the man in front of me to the laptop and then back. "You said your W2s and bank information are in there?"

"Yeah."

"So that means also your social security number?"

"Yep."

"How's your credit?"

He looked confused. "Excellent. Even my credit scores are included in there. You can take a look at them if you want."

"So pretty much I have everything I need to steal your identity?"

"Pretty much."

"Cool. Leave the laptop, and I'll call you in the morning when I'm done."

He balked, and I couldn't hold back a laugh. "I'm joking."

He gave a sigh of relief. "For a minute there, I thought you were planning on buying a condo under my name."

"Are you really that well off?"

"Yes."

"Wow, dating is really a billion dollar industry isn't it?"

He pulled me toward him, and I let him gather me in his arms. I sighed in contentment. This was exactly where I wanted to be.

"So do you forgive me?" he asked, pulling away from me just enough to see my face.

I shrugged and pretended to be unsure. "I don't know… it's going to cost you—"

"I'm willing to pay the price…"

"You sound too confident."

"I'll do anything for you. Just say you forgive me."

"I might forgive you… in a lifetime or two."

"And what am I expected to do until then?"

"Love me."

He smiled and his eyes connected with mine. "Consider it done."

ALSO BY SUMMER COOPER

DARK DESIRES
~ A billionaire dark romance series ~
Dark Desire
Dark Rules
Dark Secret
Dark Time
Dark Truth

BARRE TO BAR
~ A billionaire second chance series ~
Dancing With Lies
Dancing With Temptation
Dancing With Doubt
Dancing With Guilt
Dancing With Redemption

TWISTED INTENTION
~ A billionaire revenge romance series ~
Twisted Beauty
Twisted Love
Twisted Fate

Mafia's Obsession
~ A hot mafia romance series ~
Mafia's Dirty Secret
Mafia's Fake Bride
Mafia's Final Play

Screaming Demons
~ An MC romance series full of suspense ~
Rough Start
Rough Ride
Rough Choice
Rough Patch
Rough Return
Rough Road
Rough Trip
Rough Night
Rough Love

Standalone Contemporary Romance
Billionaire in Vegas
Billionaire Hunt

Billionaire's Game
Billionaire Retreat
Billionaire On Air
A Chance To Love
Somebody To Love
Not Mine To Love

Check out Summer's entire collection at
www.summercooper.com/books

ABOUT SUMMER COOPER

Thank you so much for reading. Without you, it wouldn't be possible for me to be a full-time author. I hope you enjoy reading my books as much as I do writing them.

Besides (obviously!) reading and writing, I also love cuddling my dogs, shouting at Alexa, being upside down (aka Yoga) and driving my family cray-cray!

Get in touch at
hello@summercooper.com
www.summercooper.com

facebook.com/summercooperauthor
instagram.com/summercooperauthor
goodreads.com/summercooper
bookbub.com/profile/summer-cooper